Dear Reader,

A single flaw almost destroyed me. You see, I believed that it was easier to marry a man who would take care of me than to take care of myself.

When my marriage to a wealthy man failed, I fled from the dangerous men who were after my ex-husband to the wild rugged wilderness of Colorado to hide on my brother's ranch. I wanted to start over, to be more than a spoiled, pampered princess-wife. I wanted a career. I was determined to resist the temptation of marrying for money again.

Then I met a rich man.

I was instantly drawn to Jake Kassidy, who was tough and hard and as rugged as the huge ranch he owned. Although he was different than the glamorous, superficial people I had known before, I suspected my motives.

Jake had his own reasons for not wanting to fall in love.

But the harder we fought our feelings, the more powerful they grew. Then the vengeful men from my past found me and threatened not only my life but my new love.

Amber Johnson

Please address questions and book requests to: Silhouette Reader Service
U.S.: 3010 Walden Ave., P.O. Box 1325, Buffalo, NY 14269
Canadian: P.O. Box 609, Fort Erie, Ont. L2A 5X3

WESTERN *Lovers*

ANN MAJOR

THE FAIRY TALE GIRL

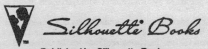

Published by Silhouette Books

America's Publisher of Contemporary Romance

To Anita Diamant,
for being not only a wonderful agent
but also a friend.

SILHOUETTE BOOKS
300 East 42nd St.,
New York, N.Y. 10017

ISBN 0-373-88521-0

THE FAIRY TALE GIRL

Copyright © 1987 by Ann Major

This edition published by arrangement with Harlequin Books S.A.

® and TM are trademarks of Harlequin Books S.A., used under license.
Trademarks indicated with ® are registered in the United States Patent
and Trademark Office, the Canadian Trade Marks Office and in other
countries.

Printed in U.S.A.

Chapter One

Amber wadded a silk suit into a ball and threw it into one of the open suitcases on her bed. Don had bought the outfit, with its matching scarves, in the Faubourg St. Honoré quarter of Paris a little over a year ago. How proudly she had worn it.

Now those memories seemed dimly remembered fantasies. Her fingers shook with fear against the cool folds of material. She had to get away, and quickly!

When the telephone shattered the early-morning silence, she grabbed for it on the first ring.

"Hello." The one word was bitten out. A frozen sound against the stillness.

"Is this Mrs. Amber Lynn?"

Amber recognized the nurse's voice at once, and her heart stopped. Then it began to beat more violently than before. The rope of pearls she'd been about to pack slid through her fingers to the floor.

"How is she?" Amber whispered, dreading the answer.

"Mrs. Lynn, I'm very sorry, but your mother died this morning. The doctors tried everything that . . ."

The cool voice was faint, blurred by static. Uncaring.

Her mother had died alone, among strangers.

Amber had been expecting the long-distance call, but now that it had come she wasn't ready. For a timeless moment she clutched the receiver against her ear and was unable to speak.

It was her fault that her mother had died. Her failure. And Don's.

Why had she always failed her mother in everything?

At last Amber managed to ask the necessary questions, and make the arrangements and decisions expected of her.

Then she hung up and walked numbly out of her hotel room, not bothering to shut the door, leaving all her belongings—even her purse with her money and airline ticket—behind her.

She walked for miles, scarcely knowing where she walked though her footsteps followed familiar pathways. At last she came to the beach, not far from the villa where she'd once lived.

Blue-gray rain clouds hovered against the horizon, though there was sunshine over the island. The aquamarine waters were eerily brilliant against this dark background. The beach was deserted; later it would be crowded with sunbathing tourists and with the glittering people who had once been Amber's friends.

A rush of cold wind swept in from the sea, ruffling the surface of the water so that it sparkled like diamonds and swirling the sand into gritty clouds that stung her cheeks and made her eyes burn. Or was it the tears she couldn't shed for her mother that made her eyes feel so hot and scratchy?

In the lush dark gardens of the rich who had houses on this beach, the trees bent low, and light and shadow danced together beneath their boughs.

The wildness of the sea and wind brought a curious comfort to Amber's troubled soul, and she stood staring out to sea, watching it shimmer and dance beneath scudding clouds. Such a spectacle her mother, who had once fancied herself a painter, would have called "the colors of the wind."

"The wind is magic, child," she used to say. "It makes everything come to life. The sun gives light. But only the wind gives us sparkle."

It was a happy memory, and there weren't many of those.

"Oh, Mother..." Amber's voice trailed away and was lost.

The old needs were still there, the terrible hunger for her mother's love that had driven Amber to make all the mistakes she'd made.

Amber started to turn back and return to her hotel. Then she stopped herself.

She couldn't go without seeing the villa again. Just one last time. For the first time since the telephone call from Denver, she remembered the danger to herself and Don, but she was too upset to care.

Avoiding the open beach, she crept beneath the tall palms and pink oleanders until she reached the garden gate that had once belonged to her. Glancing inside to see if anyone was there, she was reassured by the garden's brooding silence. She struggled with the latch and pushed the gate open.

Amber stood in silence, her gaze tracing every detail of the sun-spotted greenery with an intensity that betrayed how deeply she was affected.

Here she had loved and been loved. Or at least she had thought she had. Here she had known happiness and misery, triumph and despair. Here she had first begun to learn the true meaning of disillusion and terror.

Now she had to run away, and quickly, before it was too late. She would have to change her name. More importantly, she would have to become a completely new person.

The early-morning sunlight slanted into the garden, splashing trees and blossoms with its fiery iridescent light. Everything seemed different now, different because she was so changed, yet everything was as breathtakingly lovely as she remembered. She paused to savor the roar of the sea, the towering, rustling palms that could darken the flamboyant tapestry of the garden with deep shadows even on the most brilliant of days.

Slowly Amber latched the gate behind her, then leaned down and removed one emerald-green sandal to shake the sand from it before slipping it once more upon her slim tanned foot. As she stood up again, she stared at the graceful house crowning the scant rise above the sea. Then she looked quickly away, but not before a solitary tear trickled down her cheek.

The sugar-white villa with its lush, green garden had been her home, this mansion set in paradise, where the salty fragrance of the sea and the perfume of a thousand exotic blossoms were ever present. Now she and

Don had lost it, just as they had lost everything else, even each other. In her purse at the hotel was a one-way ticket to Colorado and a new life, a life without the glamour of her former life, but a life without the lies as well. A life without Don. A life free of perpetual fear. Their divorce was an accomplished fact, though Don still hadn't accepted it—just as the men to whom they owed so much money would not accept it. They held her responsible for what Don had done.

And they were right, in a way. Amber had grown immeasurably even to be able to acknowledge her own guilt.

It was an old story. A single flaw in one's character could ruin the fabric of one's entire life. A single defect could triumph over everything good in one's nature.

It takes but a drop of poison to contaminate the well.

Amber had been so terribly young, so foolishly young. She had made mistakes. She had hurt people, herself most of all. But at last she was beginning to understand why it had been so important to her to have things, instead of simply to be.

Her father had died when she was little more than a baby, and Amber had had only her mother, who blamed her for everything that had gone wrong in her own life. Her mother continually told her that having Amber had ruined her body and that she wished she'd never had a child at all. Not only that, but having a child had ruined her chances to catch a new man and make a new life for herself.

In time her mother had become a hypochondriac, demanding that Amber nurse her since it was pregnancy and childbirth that had ruined her health. Amber grew up with a terrible sense of guilt and a fierce craving for her mother's love and approval, but because her mother loved only herself, Amber's needs were never satisfied. Nor was she allowed to play with other children. She wanted to go to parties and be young, but the few times she managed to go out she had always felt like an outsider.

It had seemed to Amber that wonderful things happened only to other people. She'd been a dreamer who'd imagined herself a princess in a fabulous fairy tale. She'd wanted money and all the things money could buy. Maybe then her mother would admire her.

Her invalid mother had taught her that there was one sure road to success for a girl with looks. Amber had simply taken that road. She had not realized until it was too late that all she had ever really wanted was her mother's love.

"A girl needs a man. But don't forget, it's just as easy to marry a rich man as a poor man," her mother would advise. "If only your father hadn't died, and you hadn't been born, and I hadn't lost my health. It was the stress of doing for myself . . . and doing for you, Amber dear. Don't bother about a career, child. It's a much surer thing to catch a man to take care of you. And don't have a baby!"

Instead of concentrating on developing her mind, Amber had concentrated on becoming enticingly feminine.

If only she'd worked a tenth as hard on her mind! Perhaps she would have been smart enough to realize she was going after the wrong things for the wrong reasons. She might not have believed so readily in Don and his grand schemes of real estate development in the Bahamas. She might not have married him after a brief, whirlwind courtship. She might have known that trust and honor were commodities of far greater worth than money. But no, she had delighted in her new wealth when she so effortlessly received everything she had ever thought she wanted and much much more.

Don was as handsome as a magazine model, a golden, middle-aged, smooth-talking entrepreneur with needs of his own. He had needed a young beautiful wife. He'd built casinos, villas and hotels. For her he'd built Paradise Villa, this oasis of dazzling splendor amid the fake glamour of Lucaya Beach.

All he'd asked of Amber was that she wear his diamonds, entertain at his side and be his eternally youthful, eternally glamorous showcase wife.

She'd felt valued and admired as she'd never felt as a child. Perhaps that was why this sham of a marriage had been enough for her until Don's shattering revelation that he was overextended and was facing bankruptcy proceedings. There were also lawsuits pending against Lynn Construction because certain building projects had not been built to the proper specifications. And there were the men who had threatened them both if they didn't pay back the money Don had borrowed.

In the disillusioning and terrifying months that had followed, she'd learned that she and Don were strangers. All she really knew about him was that he drove a Mercedes, smoked too many cigarettes and stayed out late making deals. She'd been the exquisite pet he came home to when his real life was over. They had never really talked about anything except the people they knew and the parties they would go to.

When the threatening telephone calls began, Don made her understand that she couldn't tell anyone about them—especially not the police.

"They will kill me if you do," he had said. "They might even kill you, baby." And she had believed him.

As if there were anyone who would listen to her problems. At first after she and Don had lost everything, it was a shock to realize that she had no one. Their friends had evaporated along with the money. Her own mother had suffered a massive heart attack when she heard of Don's bankruptcy. Her last words before she'd slipped into a coma were, "Amber, you were the greatest mistake of my life."

Terrible as that pronouncement had been, there was more than a little truth in her mother's words. Amber had taken a hard look at herself and had seen a poor creature with no more substance than Don. No wonder she had no friends and no husband. She had so little faith in herself that she'd chased after dreams instead of facing reality. She'd been a child who wanted life to be easy, and suddenly she'd grown up and discovered it wasn't. Perhaps Don had represented security or the father she had never had or the mother's love she had always craved.

It didn't matter now. She was going to Denver to bury her mother—and, she hoped, the past hurts they had inflicted upon one another. Then she was going to start over. She would try to establish herself and make enough money so that she could help Don. Even though she hadn't borrowed the money herself, and in fact had known nothing about Don's business affairs, she felt responsible for what he'd done. Don agreed that she had to go.

"If you leave and I don't have to worry about what these guys might do to you, I'll be able to handle them, baby."

She was determined to make something of herself. If she ever let another man into her life—she was too badly scarred emotionally to believe she could ever marry again—she would choose a man for who he was rather than for what he could give her. And she would have to know she had something of value to give him.

While she was married to Don, she'd amused herself by dabbling in jewelry design. She'd worn her creations to her parties and been stunned when her guests had begged her to make them copies. She began to realize that she was talented. Slowly she'd grown more and more intrigued, and finally she'd begun selling a few items in a shop that belonged to one of her friends. Gradually her hobby had turned into the promise of a profession. This skill, and her tools, were the only things she would take with her into her new life.

Amber walked in the purple darkness beneath an enormous ficus tree. Weeds were sprouting in the flower beds. Once there had been gardeners to care for the grounds. Now there was a forlornness about the garden as it awaited its new owner.

The brilliant, shimmering light had turned golden. An enormous passionflower vine climbed the white walls of the villa, spilling down from the tiled roof in great garlands of exotic blue-violet flowers. On impulse, she picked a blossom and tucked it behind her ear. It was as beautiful as any jewel against the flaming tresses of her coppery hair.

The garden overflowed with trumpet vines, red bottle brush, flame vines and crape myrtle. A poinciana tree, with its long-clawed scarlet blossoms, towered beside the fountain. Amber looked into the glimmering pool of water and saw the troubled reflection of a young girl in a strapless green sundress.

Where was the exquisite beauty who had given the most wonderful parties in Nassau on Don's floating palace? Where were the jewels that had adorned her slender, majestic throat? Where was the dynamic girl-child whose bold beauty was always enhanced by designer clothes from Paris? The girl with the astonishing cascades of apricot hair? The girl who laughed at everything as she sipped champagne from shimmering Waterford goblets? The girl who thought life was a continual merry-go-round? The girl whose wide-set blue eyes were as vivid and sparkling as the sea that caressed these soft-scented islands? The fairy-tale girl who'd believed so trustingly that her dreams had come true? Surely this pale ghost in the green summer dress had nothing to do with her.

In a burst of emotion, Amber reached down and stirred the blood-warm water with her fingertips and watched as her reflection broke into a thousand fragments that were carried away on glimmering ripples. She had no desire to look into that troubled girl's doubt-filled eyes, but someday soon she would feel proud of herself again. This time, though, there would be more substance behind the image.

Arising, she left the garden and climbed the stone stairs that led to the house. Inside, she walked through the empty rooms, each grander and more pretentious than the one before. There were faded places on the walls where original oil paintings had hung. All of them were gone now, sold months ago at that humiliating auction. On the wooden facings there were fresh marks, scars left by impatient movers who'd carried away all her most highly prized possessions.

Amber's footsteps echoed like hollow heartbeats on the pink marble floors. She remembered these rooms filled with lavish furnishings, glittering people and false happiness. Now all that remained was a stack of Lynn Realty signs that had been tossed into one corner of the kitchen and forgotten. It was odd, but the new Amber almost preferred the emptiness.

Amber went to a window and lifted the curtain. One glance at the broad-shouldered man with the thick golden hair, the umber tan and the permanent grin told her it was Don. He crushed a cigarette beneath his heel, then leaned over his silver lighter to light the fresh one he'd just shaken from a nearly empty pack.

Unsteady fingers clutched the curtain. Don was the last person she wanted to see. He would want to know where she was going, and if he knew, he would eventually try to find her. He still believed that Marina del Mar would drop its ten-million-dollar lawsuit, and that soon he would have new investors and be building more white villas, more lavish hotels. Then he would be able to pay back the dangerous men to whom he owed so much money. "All this will be forgotten, baby," he always said. "I've been up and I've been down. Everything will be just like it was." And maybe he was right.

It was strange, but even if she could have it all back, she wouldn't want it now. She wanted to be more than a rich man's pampered ornament.

At least, she hoped she did. What would happen if she met a rich man who seemed to be the answer to all her problems? Would she really be strong enough to resist the temptation to marry him just for what he could do for her? Would she still equate material success with personal worth?

Suddenly she began to run. She didn't want to hear all Don's old promises again, nor did she want to be reminded of the terrible danger she was in.

She opened the sliding glass door that led onto the terrace. Filmy curtains blew in the wind as she stumbled outside.

The passionflower she'd worn in her hair fell to the ground. It blazed against the polished marble floor like a sapphire fallen from its setting, its trembling petals darkening and lightening as the wind played with their delicate edges. She ran on, not bothering to pick the flower up, even though she knew that if she left it Don would know she had been there.

She had to get away, from him, from the broken dreams that had almost destroyed her.

She left nothing of herself when she went, nothing but the fragile blossom she had picked by chance and worn briefly in her hair, an exquisite purple flower that lay fluttering on sun-warmed marble, as broken and forgotten as her dreams.

Today her mother had died.

But it was a day of endings that somehow held the promise of new beginnings.

Chapter Two

Through the open window, Amber was staring at the granite mountains that seemed to tower like white-crowned giants just beyond the shimmering sweep of pink desert, but she didn't even see them. She was thinking about a man. The best-looking man she had ever seen.

Jake Kassidy.

Only when the wind whispered his name aloud did Amber realize she had been thinking of him again.

Black hair, sparkling green eyes, white teeth. And he had a devilish grin that made him absolutely charming.

He was huge. And gorgeous. Tanned and muscled. No man alive deserved to be so good-looking.

She'd only seen him once, in town a week ago, and he hadn't even noticed her.

But he was the only man she'd noticed since Don.

Jake Kassidy was the one bachelor that Serena hadn't invited over tonight to meet her!

Didn't that prove he was no good?

But there had been such a commanding aura about him. He wasn't like Amber. He didn't chase elusive dreams. He went after what he wanted. And that was what made him dangerous.

He had gone after money and had made a great deal of it. He was the kind of man who could give a girl everything she dreamed of having. Such a girl would be admired.

Amber tore her gaze from the mountains and the desert and went back to her mirror, where she wound her damp freshly washed hair into a prim knot at the nape of her neck. She was dreading this party her half brother Hamlin and his wife Serena had insisted on giving tonight to introduce her to their rancher friends.

She had come to Colorado to hide, not to meet people, and it was against her every instinct to expose herself. She was afraid that somehow, in some way, someone would see through her disguise as plain Amber Johnson and recognize the once-glamorous Amber Lynn. She was afraid, too, that she might give in to that old temptation of hers, of seeking a man for what he could do for her. Even though her mother was dead, Amber was still filled with the same need to prove herself. Wasn't that why she kept thinking of Jake Kassidy?

"You can resist anything except temptation, my girl," Amber whispered at her reflection in the mirror. "Why, you can't even drive into town after groceries without being tempted."

But no matter how nervous she was at the prospect of the evening before her, there was no way to avoid this party without hurting Serena and Hamlin.

The barbecue was to be at seven-thirty. The immense Johnson ranch house was redolent of wood-smoke from the barbecue pits outside and the smell of beans simmering in the kitchen. Great vases filled with black-centered scarlet poppies adorned tables decked with red-and-white checkered tablecloths. Pots brimming with geraniums, petunias and pansies had been pulled onto the porch. Lanterns had been set up along the walk and the driveway, to be lit at dusk. All these preparations made Amber feel even more uncertain.

Hamlin was Amber's father's son by his first wife. who had died shortly after Hamlin's birth. Hamlin's mother had come from a wealthy family, and eventually, Hamlin had become the sole heir to his mother's vast fortune. Thus, while Amber's half brother had always been rich, she and her mother had been poor, a fact her mother had deeply resented.

Amber had been in Colorado a month now. During that time she had kept mostly to herself, working feverishly in the shop Hamlin had let her set up with her jewelry-making tools. Amber had taken back her maiden name, Johnson—the same as Hamlin's—and removed her wedding rings. She had begged Hamlin to say nothing of her former marriage, reminding him that it was a painful chapter in her life, one she wanted to close forever. She had quit wearing makeup and contact lenses and now wore the thick glasses she had always hated. She pinned her long hair into an unstylish knot, but despite her drab disguise she was always afraid she would be recognized.

Her fear had lessened somewhat. She had been able to make many new pieces of jewelry to send to her friend Angela, who owned the luxurious jewelry shop on Grand Bahama Island where Amber had sold her creations in the past. Amber used a post office box in Breckenridge so that her address was untraceable, and she had extracted a promise from Angela that she would not tell Don or anyone else that the jewelry was her creation. The jewelry was selling well, but Amber was starting from nothing. It would be a while before she could afford a place of her own, so she would have to live with Hamlin for several more months.

Serena and Hamlin had urged Amber not to work so hard. "You should be around people more," the beautiful, dark Serena would say in her husky voice. By "people" Serena meant "men." Amber had demurred, saying that for the moment her work must come first. Serena couldn't understand Amber's reticence where men were concerned—just as she couldn't understand Amber's determination to stand alone, to be self-supporting.

The thought of meeting so many strangers tonight worried Amber. She had quit working at noon and had come up to her room to begin to get ready several hours before the party. She'd bathed and washed her long hair. She'd scrubbed her face and had even decided to sterilize her soft contact lenses, just in case she decided to wear them.

After setting the lenses to sterilize in their heater, she lifted her glasses from the counter and set the heavy frames on the slender bridge of her nose. She made a face at the plain creature in the mirror, who looked like some spinster librarian destined to spend a lifetime buried behind dusty bookshelves. Better to be plain and unnoticed but alive, she thought dismally. Better to become a person than to remain an ornament.

Amber glanced at her watch. It was hours until the party. She pulled on the blue jeans and shirt she'd been working in and went downstairs to see if there was anything she could do to help Serena.

Serena was curled up on a kitchen chair studying a cookbook while Paula, her housekeeper, a plump, silver-haired replica of Mrs. Santa Claus, added onion and ham to the great pot of beans simmering on the stove.

"I was wondering if there was anything I could do," Amber asked.

Serena slammed the book closed in one of her typical agitated gestures and jumped up. "Not a thing, darling. Maybe later."

Amber caught the scent of wild roses, the fragrance Serena always wore.

"But you've done so much. So much more than I deserve."

"Nonsense." Serena lit a cigarette and inhaled deeply. She threw back her head, and Amber admired the grace of her long, slim neck. Serena was a natural beauty. She wore her raven hair in a cap of glossy curls that set off black-lashed dark eyes and a perfectly shaped scarlet mouth. She was so majestically tall that, even in the old jeans and the yellow pullover sweater she wore, she looked as if she'd just sprung from the pages of the latest fashion magazine.

Yet for all Serena's beauty and superficial friendliness, Amber never felt comfortable with her. Serena was charged with an almost frantic energy. With her only son, Dave, away at camp for the summer, Serena seemed to be constantly at loose ends. It was almost as if she were possessed of some terrible, insoluble problem. Sometimes Amber would come into a room and find Serena staring out the window with a look of the most profound loss on her face. Once she'd even asked Serena if something was wrong.

Serena had looked startled. "What could possibly be wrong? Don't I have everything a woman could want? The perfect husband, a child, our beautiful home."

The Amber of the past would have agreed with her, but the new Amber was puzzled at the tears lurking in Serena's luminous dark eyes and at her quivering smile. Beneath the surface, life was not always as wonderful as it seemed. Amber wanted to help her, but if Serena refused to confide in her, what could she do?

Hamlin was devoted to Serena. Unlike Don, he was a solid, no-nonsense rancher, a man who had no dangerous enemies.

Amber opened the refrigerator and pulled out a can of Coke. "I don't know what I'm going to say or do tonight, Serena. I've forgotten how to act around people."

"Just be yourself, darling, and everyone will discover for themselves how charming you are."

"I wouldn't feel so shy if you hadn't invited every single bachelor in three counties! What am I going to do with all those men?"

"That's the kind of problem most women would enjoy," said Serena without a trace of sympathy.

Paula had finished with the onions, and she was never one to stay out of any conversation long. "She hasn't invited quite every bachelor, dearie. There's one she should be inviting, but she won't. The most interesting one of all, if anyone's asking me."

Serena's lips thinned, and she stubbed out her half-smoked cigarette in a quick, high-strung movement.

"Well, nobody's asking you, Paula." Serena kept jabbing at the cigarette long after it was dead.

Paula had practically raised Serena, and she never minded speaking her mind on any subject. Sometimes it was difficult for Amber to remember that Serena was the older woman's employer. Watching them warily, Amber opened her Coke and began to sip it.

"It's downright rude of you, Serena, to leave him out," continued Paula. "After all, Jake Kassidy is your next-door neighbor now. Not to mention the fact that you knew him when he was a boy. Some welcome from his dearest childhood friend! And after his being gone so long!"

Jake Kassidy. The name quivered through Amber like a low charge of electricity. She found herself listening spellbound.

"He shouldn't have come back! Ever!" Serena exclaimed passionately.

"You don't own this town, dearie. And when was there anyone who could tell Jake what to do and not have him laugh in their face? Though it seems to me I remember it was you who tried. The two of you used to fight like cats and dogs when you were kids. Regular little savages, you were. But then, most of the time you got along. Never did see two kids that liked each other any better, though I didn't approve of the way your mother let you go off with him all day in the desert all the summer long. Come every evening, back you'd be with such treasures as horny toads and gopher snakes you wanted to make pets of. And she'd go out back and rustle up some sort of cage. I never saw another boy who had such a way with animals. Why, most kids his age let run wild like he was would have shot everything that moved. Not Jake. For all his roughness, he's got a gentle heart.''

"I don't know why we can't just drop Jake as a subject,'' Serena said in a choked voice.

"Because I can't stand by while you deliberately snub him.''

"I'm not snubbing him.'' Serena lit another cigarette and began to pace back and forth in front of the windows that looked out upon blue mountains. "People change, Paula, and not always for the best. Jake bought that ranch for a fraction of what it was worth. Bill Chandler was our friend. He wouldn't have sold it if he hadn't been desperate. How can I feel anything but hostile toward a man who took advantage of my friend?''

"Jake just bought the ranch. From what I hear, the Chandlers are mighty grateful to him.''

"Jake should have stayed in Denver where he belongs!''

"Who's to say where anyone belongs? This is his home same as it's yours, dearie.''

Amber shivered as she remembered Jake Kassidy. The name alone conjured the now-familiar image of boldness and carved, dark masculinity. She'd been hanging on every word of the argument, her blood thrumming with a mysterious hot intensity. How could Serena hate such a man? How could any woman? Even a woman like herself, who knew too well the danger of succumbing to outward charm? Or was he so fascinating to her only because of his obvious wealth and power? A man like Jake Kassidy could do a lot for a woman who wasn't woman enough to do for herself.

Amber didn't hear Serena's acidic retort. She was remembering something that had puzzled her last Saturday morning, when she and Serena had driven the Jeep into town to buy groceries for the party. Serena's behavior had baffled her at the time, and Amber had found herself dwelling on it again and again when she was alone working on her jewelry. Somehow it had become a pleasant occupation to think of Jake Kassidy, even if Serena did dislike him, even if Amber's own fascination did seem linked to the old flaw in her character that had brought about her downfall. At least Jake was a distraction from the terrifying past that Amber was fighting so hard to put behind her.

Serena and Amber's shopping trip had been uneventful until they'd finished buying their groceries and had climbed into the front seat of the Jeep while the bag boy stuffed their bulging sacks into the back. The boy had finished, and Serena had been giving him a generous tip when the door of a blue pickup truck parked next to their Jeep had swung open, and a tall dark man had climbed out of it.

"Serena," came the deep velvet tone of the stranger.

There was such sensuous beauty in that husky male voice that Amber had longed to hear her own name so caressed.

"Jake...I..." The usually poised Serena had looked quickly away from the handsome stranger and tried frantically to plunge her keys into the ignition. In her haste, she dropped them on the floorboard.

"Damn! They've gone under your seat, Amber. Could you reach them for me?"

Amber leaned down and retrieved the keys.

"Looks like you bought enough to feed an army, Serena," the man said easily. "What's the occasion?" When Serena only looked at him desperately, he went on. "I knew sooner or later we were bound to run into one another again. You couldn't hide out there on your ranch forever."

"Jake, most people would take a hint if they thought someone was trying to avoid them."

"You should know better than anybody, I'm not most people."

Serena grabbed a cigarette and lighter from the dashboard. The stranger moved forward and took the lighter from her trembling fingers so that he could light her cigarette. He leaned inside the car.

For the first time, Amber saw him clearly as she squinted through her thick glasses. The sunlight glinted on his raven-black hair and blazed in his piercing jade-green eyes. Those eyes, eyes too beautiful for such a ruggedly male face as his, were starred with the densest curling black lashes Amber had ever seen. Yet there was nothing feminine about his eyes. They were bold with the hint of insolent humor. At the moment, though, he seemed to be trying to suppress their boldness.

He was as swarthy as a Gypsy and as handsome as a pirate. He had a long, thin nose with flaring nostrils and a wide, sensual mouth. Once, when he glanced past Serena into the semidarkness of the jeep toward Amber, his indifferent gaze left her curiously breathless, and it was difficult to imagine why Serena considered this stranger so repulsive. Despite her determination to have nothing more to do with the male sex, Amber would have given anything if he had found her as interesting as he obviously found Serena. Amber even wished she hadn't worn her glasses and that her hair hadn't been pinned back in such an unflattering style.

Up to your old tricks, aren't you, girl? a small silent voice taunted Amber. The minute you spot a man to latch on to, he becomes a target. It's as easy to tempt you as it is to tease a cat with a string.

Amber tried not to look at Jake again, but like the cat with the string, she could not resist the temptation.

Jake's was an easy, irresistible charisma. His frequent smiles were so devastating they made Amber shiver, even though it was a warm sunny morning. He was the kind of man that, seen once, no woman could ever forget.

Especially a woman who has uses for such a man, the secret voice goaded.

It wasn't the power of the man, Amber thought guiltily. It was simply the man himself.

Amber found herself savoring every detail of his presence, especially his voice. It made her think of moonlight and velvet whispers in warm darkness. She was suddenly aware of how long it had been since she'd been in a man's arms. But even when she'd been married, she'd never ached with longing as she did now. And he'd scarcely looked at her! Only this irritating thought snapped her out of the schoolgirl delirium he had so effortlessly aroused. She was through with men—at least for now!

What was there about him? Suddenly, and with new annoyance both at herself and at him, Amber stared hard at Jake. Was he really so different from all the other men she'd encountered this past year?

He wore jeans and black sharkskin boots. Surely there was nothing special in that. A pale-green work shirt he'd left partially unbuttoned at the throat stretched across the broad expanse of his muscled shoulders.

Amber inhaled deeply. What was it that made her notice the way the color of his shirt deepened the color of his eyes?

Jake, she thought idly, Jake with the jade-green eyes.

He was beautiful. Deliciously, sinfully beautiful.

Amber forced herself to look away. What if he saw her gaping at him? He'd think her a silly little man-starved fool, which was exactly what she was.

"Jake, you never did know when to leave well enough alone," Serena was saying bitingly.

"I just want to be your friend, Serena. Is that a crime?"

"Maybe. When I don't want to have anything to do with you."

"I'm going to find a way to make you change your mind."

"Look, Jake, I've got to go. My ice cream will melt. Hamlin's expecting me. We'll see you around some-time."

At Serena's abrupt dismissal his smile vanished, and Amber found herself feeling sorry for him. She fought back the urge to utter some kind word to make his look of hurt go away. As if he would care what she said! As if that weren't the oldest trick in the book to make a man notice a woman!

"Sure, Serena." He nodded grimly. "See you around. I'm determined on that." There was some-thing almost threatening in his low voice.

He stepped back as Serena started the Jeep. Then she left him in a cloud of dust.

Amber stared after him. She'd never seen Serena be-have so rudely. "Who was he?" she ventured at last.

"Oh, just someone I knew once. A long, long time ago," said Serena in a strange, tight voice that wasn't her own at all.

"Someone you wish you'd never known." Amber was thinking of Don as she said that.

"You pegged it, Amber darling."

"He's quite handsome."

"Some people might think so. If they go for conceited, bullying, overbearing types. Which I don't."

"Is he rich?" Oh, why had she had to know that last? It was but more proof that the defect in her makeup had not been entirely corrected.

"Extremely...now. There was a time, you see, when he had nothing. There were people who thought he was rough and hard. They looked down on him like he was dirt."

"Oh, I see."

"Stay away from him, darling. He's not your sort."

"What do you mean?"

"You've already had your heart broken once, Amber darling. Jake has never married, but he's not the kind to do without women either, I can assure you. He's only interested in one thing, and that's never going to be marriage. He'd use you and discard you. I think you have enough emotional damage from your divorce to contend with, without someone like Jake taking a battering ram to your ego."

Put in that light, Jake Kassidy should have seemed less attractive. Serena certainly sounded as if she were speaking from experience.

"Did he deliberately hurt some friend of yours or something, Serena?"

"Well, maybe not deliberately, but she was hurt just the same."

After that, Amber had not dared to break the silence that fell between them. Besides, she didn't want to appear too interested in that handsome snake.

But Amber did notice that Serena had been especially nervous this past week, ever since she had seen Jake in town. Though Amber was burning with curiosity to know more about the man, she was too thoughtful to mention him again. Serena hadn't either, until Paula forced her to.

The smell of beans burning in the kitchen snapped Amber out of her reverie.

"Well," Paula growled at Serena, "see what you nearly made me do, exasperating me by being so bullheaded, Serena? I nearly went and ruined dinner."

"I'd say it's high time we turned our minds to more worthwhile things than Jake Kassidy," Serena retorted in her crispest, most superior tone.

"Since there's no changing your stubborn mind once it's set, I'll agree to that," said Paula, relenting. "But I'm right, you know. I'll bet it's lonely for Jake, being new in town, out there all by himself on that ranch."

"Maybe if he gets lonely enough he'll oblige us by leaving."

Amber finished her Coke and tossed the can into the garbage. "If the two of you don't mind, I think I'll borrow Golden and go for a short ride."

"Go right ahead, darling. And take Golden some carrots for me, will you?" Serena said, pulling two from a nearby tray and handing them to Amber.

"I peeled those carrots," Paula cried.

"Golden doesn't mind peeled carrots," Serena purred.

"It's me that minds peeling them...for a horse," said Paula. Serena only glared at Paula without relinquishing the carrots. "Well, I never!" Paula grumbled.

Though the discussion about Jake was over, it was obvious that neither woman had forgotten it. It was going to be a long, difficult afternoon, and as she slammed the storm door behind her, Amber was glad she was getting out of the house.

The pungent scent of sage and juniper filled the air. Goldenrod quivered in the faint breeze.

Amber was oblivious to her surroundings. As she raced to the barn, she was still thinking about what had been said in the kitchen.

Jake Kassidy. She'd never even spoken to him, but he had stolen her imagination against her will. She envisioned him out on his ranch, all alone, the only bachelor in the county Serena had not invited to her party.

She knew what it was to be friendless and alone, and though it was ridiculous to waste pity on a man who was no doubt a loathsome cad, she couldn't stop her heart from going out to him.

Perhaps he was chased by demons fiercer than her own.

Or was she only interested in him because he was the kind of man the old Amber would have wanted?

Was there really a new Amber at all?

Whatever else she did, she was determined to leave Jake Kassidy strictly alone.

Chapter Three

Amber had ridden for over an hour, her binoculars bouncing against her breast. Every day she grew to love the untamed landscape of Hamlin's ranch more.

At first she had thought the ranch's wildness desolate. Now the vivid red hills and distant mountains seemed exactly the kind of country for a person who wanted to disappear forever. Perhaps soon the scent of sage and juniper would seem as familiar as once the smell of the Atlantic had.

Oh, she hoped she would come to love this high country as once she had loved her tropical paradise. She wanted to forget everything that had gone before the new life she was determined to build for herself. But it was difficult. Sometimes she felt she would never be able to help Don. Sometimes she felt so lonely and frightened she wanted to cry. On those occasions she dreamed of finding some new Don who would make life easy again. She wanted to be petted and protected. But then she would remember the danger of such longings, of such dependence on a man.

Oh, what was it she wanted, exactly? What was the name for the emptiness in her heart that was an anguish more profound than her terror of the past?

Amber heard the gurgle of a stream and realized she'd never ridden quite this far before. Golden, sensing her rider's distraction, paused and jerked her head so hard that Amber lost the reins. The mare gave a triumphant snort of delight and began to nibble at a plump tuft of dusty grass. Amber tugged and tugged, but she couldn't pull Golden's head up.

"You're half mule! You know that, Golden!" Golden continued to gobble. "All mule!"

Amber sighed. Perhaps Golden did have the right idea. Amber slid from the saddle and led Golden toward the stream. Leaning down, she dampened her face and neck with the surprisingly warm water. She vaguely remembered Serena having said something about a hot spring.

Amber decided that if she was going to rest, she would ride up to the top of a nearby ridge, where she would at least have a view.

On the top of the ridge, she tied Golden to a juniper branch and scrambled higher by herself until, on the edge of a cliff, she found an immense boulder that provided shade. As she gazed at the mountains, she felt tiny and insignificant against such immense silent grandeur.

She studied a great fluff of cloud that peeked over one blue-shadowed mountain. Then her attention was diverted to a tiny speck, trailed by a plume of dust, that was moving across the desert with great determination toward the same stream where she'd so recently bathed her face. She sat down in the shade and focused her binoculars against her thick glasses.

Through the lenses she saw a dark man riding a powerful white horse. It was obvious that he'd been born knowing more about riding than she would ever learn, even if she spent the rest of her life in the saddle. Horse and man seemed to be of one flesh as they flew gracefully across lavender-pink desert. They quickly grew larger, and it wasn't long before they arrived at a place close to the spot where she had stopped. The man dismounted where the stream widened into a pool partially enclosed by juniper.

He was none other than Jake Kassidy!

Her hands began to tremble, and his bold male image wavered. She set the binoculars down against the faded denim covering her thigh.

Oh, it was wrong to spy on him!

She sat there for what seemed an eternity, miserably chewing a nail to bits while her conscience reigned triumphant. Why was it so dull being good?

Unbidden crept the thought: If she looked, he would never know. He didn't own the desert, now did he?

It never occurred to her that she had no inkling where she was, and that this might be Jake's ranch and not Hamlin's.

She simply itched to know what Jake was doing down there.

It is always difficult to stick to a virtuous principle in the face of temptation, especially when one thinks there is no danger of being caught.

Amber lifted her binoculars with relish. What she saw made her heart pound as fast as a rabbit's!

He was stripping.

Off came one black sharkskin boot, followed quickly by its mate. He rolled down his socks, and she feasted upon long brown feet with long narrow toes. Her binoculars were so powerful she could actually watch him wiggle his toes in the soft sand at the water's edge.

She drew a quick sharp breath. It wasn't so bad, what she was doing. Was there a law against looking at naked feet? Even when they belonged to a man as tantalizingly attractive as Jake Kassidy?

He began to unbutton his white shirt, and she watched as brown fingers flew downward, leaving in their wake an ever lengthening strip of dark furred chest. He shrugged off the shirt and tossed it on a rock near his boots.

At the sight of so much bronzed muscle, as hard as sculptured steel, she felt a wondrous shame of pure sensuousness. Her eyes moved downward, and she could not stop herself from shivering with admiration at the lean power of his athletic physique. He was beautiful as only a man can be beautiful. His broad shoulders tapered to a narrow waist, slim hard hips, and long muscular legs.

Her attention was riveted to the tanned hand unfastening his silver and turquoise belt buckle. With a gasp, she watched etched leather slide through denim belt loops. In another second he would take off his jeans!

She dropped the binoculars and sat back against the rock, flushed and breathless with excitement and guilt.

Remorse at what she had just done swept her. She had no right to invade his privacy like that. What if she saw him in town again with Serena? She would be so mortified she wouldn't be able to speak.

If only she were safely back in her bedroom. If only she had never left the ranch house. But she didn't dare leave before Jake did because he might see her slipping down from the ridge. It would scarcely take a genius to figure out who she was. He had only to ask around.

No, she was trapped until he decided to leave himself.

Though she didn't look through her binoculars again, Amber remained disturbingly aware of him as he swam in the crystal-clear pool. He must have been born with a beaver's love for the water. Once in, it seemed the man had no wish to get out.

Great splashes erupted from the pool. Damnation! Was he going to swim forever? As if in answer, she caught a glimpse of a long bronzed leg breaking the surface of the water, and another great geyser sparkled in the dazzling sunlight. It seemed he was.

She lay back against the warm rock and closed her eyes. It wasn't long before her head lolled and her thoughts dimmed as she faded into a dreamworld where a tall, gypsy-dark man emerged from a shimmering pool with wet black hair and water glistening on his lean body. His green eyes swept her appraisingly. His chest moved near and she tried to push him away, but it was like pushing living, sun-warmed granite that had been only half-cooled by a summer shower. He crushed her to him, and yet there was infinite gentleness in his embrace. She was aware of his velvet mouth moving across her skin as he sought the delicate curve of her lips. She jerked away to avoid the tantalizing temptation of his kiss, and her head fell against the stone, awakening her.

Her flesh tingled from forbidden sensual urges. She ran her fingers shakily over her mouth. It was a shock to realize that she wanted him, this Jake Kassidy with the cocky grin and the bold green eyes, this man Serena had warned her to avoid, this man who was the very type to appeal to the terrible weakness in her character.

Cold reality seeped into her mind. The man was a stranger, and she should not think such thoughts about him. Besides, she could not allow herself to become involved with any man, certainly not until she had helped Don, and not until she was sure of herself as a person in her own right. Never again, she vowed to herself, would she dream of Jake Kassidy. This one lapse was her punishment for having watched him when she shouldn't.

Fully awake now, she gazed down at the pool only to discover that horse and man were gone. She scanned the horizon in alarm but, apart from a solitary red-tailed hawk making lazy circles high above her, she saw nothing but the vastness of the empty desert.

Just as she was trying to decide whether to wait a little longer to be sure he was gone, the teasing huskiness of a man's voice came from behind the boulder.

"Serena, I know you're there. I've seen Golden. She's practically eaten a bush, the poor darling. You might as well come out now. Binoculars and all."

Amber's throat went dry; her palms moistened with nervous perspiration.

Binoculars and all! Oh, dear Lord! It was Jake, and he knew she'd been watching him. Only he didn't know who she really was. He thought she was Serena.

What in the world was she going to do?

"Serena," came the bold invitation of that silken voice again. "Are you coming out?"

Not if she could help it!

Blood pounded in her head in a series of frightened staccato drumbeats spelling danger. "Just a minute," she rasped in a feeble attempt to mimic her sister-in-law's perpetually husky voice.

"You sound like you have a cold."

"I'm okay," she snapped irritably.

Oh, what was she going to do? She glanced over the cliff's edge and saw nothing but sheer rock and weeds. Could she possibly escape him if she went down that way and hid until he grew bored and left?

"I knew sooner or later you'd get over your unfriendliness, Serena, and decide to pay me a neighborly visit."

A neighborly visit!

Oh, why did the mere sound of his voice make her tremble with a new emotion that had nothing to do with fear?

"You did?" She began to inch down the side of the cliff, holding on to a juniper branch as she struggled downward.

"But I never realized you'd take your binoculars and spy on me at our favorite old swimming hole. Tell me, did you enjoy the view?"

Damn the impertinence of the devil!

"The mountains are nice," she replied icily. Just then her foot slipped, but she grabbed hold of a rock in the nick of time.

"You know I wasn't talking about the mountains."

"Then I can't imagine what you are talking about," she said primly, hoping he wouldn't catch the breathless note in her voice.

"Liar. I was down there stark naked and looked up and saw the sunlight flash on your binoculars. And you weren't looking at the mountains. Not that I blame you."

"I was!" she cried, forgetting to use Serena's voice. This obviously indefensible falsehood on her part so agitated her that she lost her footing and began to tumble down the sheer face of rock, cactus and juniper. She kicked and clawed wildly, one kicking foot dislodging something soft and scaly from a shady niche in the rocks. She kept falling with no knowledge of what this ominous creature was.

Just when she thought there was no saving herself, the toe of her boot found a solid ledge; her bloodied hands clung tightly to a mixture of thorny weeds and rocks.

For a long moment she could do nothing but breathe raggedly while her heart pounded with fear.

Then from between her sprawled legs came the furious hiss of a snake.

Stark terror turned her body to quivering jelly as she looked down and saw an angry rattler writhing whiplike as it recoiled so it could strike her.

The snake seemed to be moving in slow motion, but, of course, it wasn't slow motion at all.

"Oh, dear God..." she murmured, freezing in terror.

"Don't pray, girl!" commanded an all-knowing male voice from above. "Kick the bastard off the cliff! Now!"

Without thinking, she obeyed the voice, and the brown scaly head lunging toward her leg missed her by a fraction of an inch, biting viciously into empty air instead of her flesh as she kicked at it again and again.

For one horrible instant her leather toe caught the reptile under its belly, and the rattler dangled in deadly balance from the tip of her boot before she managed to shake it loose. Even after it plunged over the edge of the cliff, Amber continued to scream, still kicking.

"He's gone, child. No use now yelling like an idiot and kicking at nothing."

The insolence in the man's voice turned Amber's hysteria to rage.

She'd fallen down a cliff and nearly been bitten by a snake—she who from the cradle had feared anything that slithered, not to mention heights. Even now when she was still shaking with relief and fear, she was clinging to the side of a cliff that was so sheer a mountain climber would have had reservations about tackling it.

Through crooked glasses and wisps of tangled apricot hair, she glanced up at the black-haired demon who was obviously enjoying tormenting her.

He was lucky she didn't have a gun, because she might have plugged him right between his eyes.

"How dare you make fun of me, you yellow-bellied coward," she screamed. "Why, a real man would have climbed down here and... and..."

"Let the snake bite us both." Black brows arched mockingly above brilliant eyes. "That rattler didn't look too inviting from up here. Besides, I've always been afraid of heights."

She dared to glance down at the desert floor and was suddenly dizzy.

"You coward."

"I would think you'd be more interested in flattering me than in gloating over the flaws in my character," he said, flashing her one of his infuriating smiles as he knelt above her at the cliff's edge.

"I wouldn't flatter you if my life depended on it."

"Oh, really?" The cocky grin widened. "And just how do you intend to scramble up here to safety, little one?"

"What are you saying?"

"I'm saying that this is one...er...yellow-bellied coward who has more pleasant things to do than waste his time listening to a wasp-tongued old maid with a quaint appetite for voyeurism blacken his character."

"Wasp-tongued old maid!" she cried, stung.

"Goodbye, little one."

"Goodbye? You can't leave me here."

"Just watch me." He stood up and wiped the dust from his jeans so carelessly that a few particles sprinkled down into her hair.

"You wouldn't go without pulling me up, would you?"

"I sure as hell would. Maybe a few hours alone out on that ledge will sweeten your disposition. It's worth a try. Who knows, maybe someone else will ride by that you can spy on."

"I don't want to spy on anyone else!"

"So it's only me you're so taken with."

"Ooooh! That's absurd, you loathsome braggart."

He chuckled. "Then I won't stay where I'm not wanted."

He disappeared, and she heard his heavy tread growing fainter. He really was leaving!

Her fury was stronger than ever, but at the thought of being left she swallowed her pride and yelled after him with all her might, "Jake Kassidy, you come back here." The footsteps paused. He was waiting. She softened her voice. "Maybe I was wrong..."

"Yes?" he taunted.

"Maybe I was wrong a while ago when I called you a...yellow-bellied coward."

"Only maybe?"

"I was wrong, damn it!" she screeched.

Two seconds later his glossy black head appeared over the cliff's edge. "That didn't sound like much of an apology, but maybe it's all you're capable of."

She had to bite her tongue, but somehow she managed to smile contritely.

Laughing at this crooked effort on her part, he lay down over the edge of the cliff. "This is going to get my shirt awfully dirty, little one. I do hope you're going to make this worth my while."

Worth his while... With gritted teeth, she chewed on that phrase. No wonder Serena despised the man!

He leaned down. His broad brown palm closed over her tiny white one. She was fleetingly aware of his warmth, of his incredible strength.

"Easy, little one. I'm not going to let you fall."

Even though the man was despicable, it was amazing how safe and secure she felt now that her fate was in his hands. Slowly he helped her drag herself up the cliff face until he was able to swing her effortlessly into his arms. For a long moment she stood, collapsed against the hard muscle and sinew of his powerful male body.

"Safe at last," he murmured dryly, still holding her close.

It was difficult to remember how obnoxious he was as she allowed her soft body to curve against the tough length of his. She felt the pleasant ripple of his muscles beneath his cotton shirt.

He was strong, but there was gentleness in his strength. His touch was feather-light. He smelled of leather and horses and of the juniper-perfumed stream. She felt his maleness in every fiber of her body, and it was a delicious, heady sensation that quickened something vital and exciting deep within her.

Her pulse skittered erratically. It seemed that all her life she had ached to be held as he was holding her. Never, even with Don, had she felt so wondrously cared for.

Curiously, the more she found herself delighting in him, the more determined she became to remember how she disliked him.

Jake was so good-looking that every woman he touched probably melted against him, just as she was doing. What must he be thinking? Did he find it amusing that he could quell her fury so easily? Was he used to turning wildcats into doves simply by handling them so gently?

Dear Lord, what was happening to her? Feeling more and more the fool, she tried to push him away. Just for an instant, he tightened his grip as though he were reluctant to release her, and she was aware of his power as she struggled against him.

With a little moan, she begged, "Please . . ."

He let her go.

"And just when we were both beginning to enjoy one another."

Startled, she looked into his piercing eyes. Words of denial sprang to her lips, but his sardonic smile told her he knew the truth better than she.

Why did she betray herself by letting her gaze linger on the sensual curve of his mouth? Why did she wonder how those lips would feel against naked skin? Would they turn flesh to jelly? Would they be brutal or tender?

She jerked her eyes from his mouth. He reached up to touch her hair and pulled a bobby pin free from the silken mass of orange tangles. "I'm sure you don't want to lose this little miracle worker."

She snatched the pin from him, realizing suddenly what a fright she must look. Glasses, no makeup, her hair in a wildly tangled knot. No wonder he'd laughed at her. What had he called her? Hadn't his exact words been ''a wasp-tongued old maid''? She cringed inwardly and tried to back away, but as she shifted her weight to her left foot, a hot wave of pain traveled up her leg with the speed of lightning.

Even before she cried out, strong arms were enveloping her once more to prevent her from falling. ''You're hurt.''

There was gentleness in the deep voice she kept telling herself she should hate.

He helped her limp to a nearby rock where she could sit down. ''Let me take a look at your ankle.''

''Oh, that's not necessary.''

''What if that snake grazed you with its fangs?'' he demanded with genuine concern as he knelt in front of her.

His large brown hands moved over her leg. Torn denim couldn't ward off the scorching fire of his touch. ''Tell me where it hurts,'' he commanded softly.

Her breath caught in her throat at the pressure of his fingers as they removed her shoe and then slid inside her jeans and pressed warm flesh.

How could callused fingertips on the sole of her foot be so erotic? His skilled hands traveled upward from her slender ankle over the curve of her calf. Every sense flamed alive, and she felt the blood rush to her face. She couldn't possibly let him continue. What if he realized how he affected her?

''Don't touch me!'' she gasped, her voice shaking at the traitorous response of her body. ''I can't stand it!''

He removed his hands and clenched his fists rigidly against his thighs. "All right, damn it! You do it! I don't know why I bothered with you anyway. You don't know how to act face-to-face with another human being, do you? I should have guessed that a woman who had to spy on a man with binoculars would have *some* problem. And lady, you sure do!"

Embarrassment washed over her as she watched him rise, his dark face hard. He had been being so nice.

She scarcely thought as she reached for his hand. Her eyes were downcast as she murmured hoarsely, "Jake, I'm sorry. I didn't mean..." The rest of her words caught miserably in her throat, but he seemed to understand.

He knelt again quickly. "I hurt you, didn't I, when I touched you?"

She nodded, despising herself for the lie. Better, though, that he thought it pain that made her tremble than the baffling emotion he had aroused.

"It's obvious you shouldn't put any weight on that leg until we can examine it properly. I'm taking you back to my house. Then I'll drive you over to Dr. Mason's place so he can take a quick look."

"Oh, I can't do that! I've got to get home immediately. If you'll just help me onto my horse—"

"Out of the question," he decreed, with the brash confidence of a dyed-in-the-wool male chauvinist.

Before she could protest, he leaned down and lifted her into his arms. Again she knew the shivery excitement of being held against his great male body. How thin the clothes seemed that lay between her skin and his. She could feel his heart thudding where her ear was pressed against soft cotton. She could feel the play of his muscles as he carried her, and it was dangerously pleasant being in his arms.

Instead of helping her mount Golden, he spoke a few gentle words into the twitching ear of his great white stallion. Then he lifted Amber behind his own saddle. That done, he strode to Golden and attached a long rope to her bridle. A minute later, leather creaked as he slid his long, narrow boot into the stirrup and swung himself effortlessly into the saddle in front of Amber.

"I'm not sure you could manage Golden with your bad ankle," he said by way of explanation. "And if you don't want to fall off, you'd better put your hands around my waist."

She reached gingerly around him.

"You're going to have to hold on tighter than that."

He grasped her trembling fingers, and placed them upon the firm, warm flesh of his belly.

She stiffened so that he wouldn't guess how even the most innocent contact with his body affected her.

But he guessed anyway. "Is it fear of me or of my horse that makes you so skittish, little one?"

"Your horse," she rasped.

"You mustn't let him know that, you know. He's like me, you see. There's nothing that gives Frisco more pleasure than a little power."

"I'll try to remember that," she managed shakily.

"Now lean forward and really hold me."

When she edged closer, her breasts pressed into his back. She drew a sharp little inward breath as the hard warmth of him made her nipples harden.

"That's better," he murmured.

Her parted thighs aligned themselves against his.

"Much better," he whispered, before nudging Frisco into a slow walk.

She said nothing. She merely clung to him, feeling shyly embarrassed by the way every intimacy with him made her tingle with unwanted sensations. She saw little of the countryside on the long ride to his home because she was too conscious of the horse's movements jogging his taut body against the softness of hers, too conscious as well of how alone they were, one man and one woman, in the vast flaming beauty of scarlet desert beneath towering, pink-fringed thunderheads and purple mountains.

By the time they reached the sleek rambling ranch house that was his home, the sky blazed with orange, pink and lavender.

As he lifted her from the saddle, he let her body slide the length of his. Gasping, she tried to spring free of him, but the minute she put weight on her ankle she stumbled. With a chuckle, he drew her once more into his arms.

"What's so funny?" she asked.

"I was just thinking that even yellow-bellied cowards can play the hero and ride off with the girl into the sunset."

She laughed gently. "I should never have called you that. It was just that I was so mad."

"You get mad awful quick, little one."

"You deliberately teased me."

"So I did. But I had to do something to snap you out of your hysteria."

"Oh, so that's going to be your excuse."

"Well, I had to come up with something to say to redeem myself in your eyes. You see, I'm in the mood to play the hero now."

The setting sun tinged his black hair with fire and bathed his dark features with its soft, pink light. His eyes were holding hers with such quiet intensity that she was breathless.

"What do you mean?"

"Only this."

Even before his lips grazed hers, she began to tremble.

"No, no," she whispered in fright, as she realized his intention and tried to back away.

Ignoring her words, he only caught her shoulders and brought her closer. "I keep remembering that you were spying on me when I was swimming. I thought I'd give you the opportunity to do more than look. It's much more fun, you know."

The bold heat in his eyes made her heart throb more fiercely.

One of his hands cupped her chin. His thumb traced the delicate line of her jaw and then brushed, ever so lightly, the sensuous sweetness of her pouting lips.

"Jake, no!" she gasped. "I'm sorry I watched you. Sorry if I embarrassed you."

"Oh, I'm not embarrassed."

"Well, I am."

"Are you? I'm not so sure. I keep wondering why you shiver every time I touch you."

"Let me go," she begged. Even as she said the words, she was aware of the wakening desires in her own body.

With one hand, he removed her glasses. "You don't really want me to let you go."

His mouth closed over hers just as she began to struggle. He wrestled her arms away, pulling her so tightly against his chest that their bodies seemed glued to one another.

Her heart was pounding wildly as he murmured endearments and stroked her softly. Oh, he knew too well how to rouse a woman.

He ran his fingers through tangled apricot-silk curls, smoothing a gleaming strand down around her neck where his hands halted, almost encircling her throat. His fingertips moved lower as he explored the voluptuous curves of her breasts, the tininess of her waist.

And she stood perfectly still, like a statue, tortured by the exquisite delight of broad warm hands that shaped her body to fit the tough contours of his own. He was giving her something she'd wanted for a long time.

Amber's mouth went dry, and the pink tip of her tongue appeared to run provocatively over her full red lower lip.

"You're beautiful," he murmured in amazement, watching the tantalizing curl of her tongue as he pulled her closer to him, "despite the trouble you take not to be." His breath was like a warm caress before he kissed her again.

Her half-closed lids opened and she moaned with sensuous pleasure. This time his mouth took hers fiercely, conquering any will she might have had to resist the arrogant skill of his blistering lips. He gripped her arms so hard it hurt, but she was past caring as she surrendered to the sweet tide of rapture his molten mouth evoked.

Then, suddenly, he released her, and she fell back a step, gazing in shock at the dark handsomeness of his face.

What was she doing? She wanted him. It was as if he answered some deep unnamed need that she'd had all her life. He touched some vital part of her that she'd always kept hidden, even from herself.

The glittering fire of the sun painted his features with fiery light. He seemed a stranger, and when he reached out and touched her breast, she shrank from this intimacy with him. Realizing the danger of him, she stumbled toward the house in a vain effort to escape, ignoring the pain in her ankle. Whether she was running from herself or from him, she never knew.

For a moment he stood, watching her agitated movements with the keen attention of a predator. Then he broke into a run and chased after her.

He caught her when she reached the porch and pulled her to him. "You don't want to run," he muttered hoarsely. "You were watching me at the pool because you want me." Then he kissed her in the same frightening manner as before.

Oh, why hadn't it occurred to her that he might find it provocative that she had spied on him? Why hadn't she considered the consequences of her rash misdeed?

She writhed to escape him, but he was so powerful her efforts only helped him mold her soft body more closely against his. He was shaking as he held her, his breath as harshly irregular as her own.

He pushed her against the stone wall of the house, his body pressing into hers, and kissed her harder and more deeply until she could scarcely breathe. His hands were in the flaming waves of her hair, and pins rained down onto the painted plank flooring. He kissed her again and again, as if it had been an eternity since he'd had a woman. At last he buried his face in her hair with a groan, and even this sent a tremor through her.

When his hand slid under her knees and he lifted her into his arms, she did not resist. She was vaguely aware of his opening the front door, of his heavy steps resounding on the stairs as he climbed them and bore her to his immense bedroom.

He laid her on top of a burgundy spread and then covered her with his body. Amber lay looking up at him, terrified, and yet wildly excited. His hands began tenderly to explore her body, roaming from the button tips of her ripe breasts down to her waist and gently swelling hips.

He unbuttoned her blouse and knelt to kiss the satin creaminess of her skin. When she was quaking with pleasure, he stood up and began to remove his clothes.

"You won't need your binoculars for this, little one," he said gently.

She watched him, mesmerized. He undressed in the same order as he had before. First came the tall black boots, then his shirt. But this time she didn't look away when the carved belt fell to the floor and he began to remove his snugly fitting jeans.

She noted the strip of black hair that ran from his furred chest down the length of his belly to curl around...

She jerked her eyes away, but they returned to watch in breathless need, shamelessly savoring every magnificent inch of him. He was as beautiful as a Greek god carved in marble. Only he was made of sleek, living muscle covered by flesh as brown as the darkest shade of teak except for...

Suddenly she blushed and snapped her eyes shut.

He was a stranger! How could she devour him so hungrily with her gaze? Why did it feel so profoundly right to be with him?

Her fingernails raked the thick burgundy quilting. What was she doing?

Never in all her life had anything like this happened to her. She, who was determined to have nothing to do with any man, was awash with desire for a man she hardly knew, even though deep inside she knew such passion was wrong. How had things gone so far? So quickly? She didn't know. She knew only that she had to find a way to stop him. To stop herself before it was too late.

When he came to her, he was too impassioned to sense her new terrified mood.

She could feel the eager trembling in his fingers as he began to undress her, the eager trembling of her own treacherous body.

She began to fight to elude him, but as he pushed her down onto the bed, she felt his hands on her rounded breasts, his mouth on her white throat where her pulse throbbed so unevenly. Her flesh felt cold, and then hot, as wave after wave of fire burned through her at the intimate touch of his hands.

She struggled, fighting him desperately, fighting herself even more desperately.

"Please, don't," she cried futilely.

He scarcely heard her. His mouth pressed down upon hers, and when she twisted her head upon the pillow he followed her relentlessly.

She was trembling with fear, but not only with fear. No man, not even Don in the first days of their marriage, had ever made her feel so passionately female, so wantonly in need.

How she longed to lift her arms around his muscled shoulders, to let her fingertips brush the soft black hair on his neck, to give in to the passion sweeping her with the power of a tidal surge.

She moved convulsively beneath him. He lowered his body, covering her completely. With a groan, he moved her thighs apart.

His mouth claimed hers as he tried to still her fears with the gentleness of his soft kisses.

"No!" she wept, even as she felt she was dying for him.

He merely kissed her tear-dampened cheeks as he began again to undress her.

She had to stop him! She had to!

Without knowing what she did, her hand came up and struck him so hard across the face that her palm rang with pain.

When he drew his head back, she winced at the vivid mark on his dark cheek and gave a little cry of despair. She didn't want to hurt him. She wanted only to love him.

His eyes burned fiercely as shock and anger surged through him, replacing his passion. He grabbed her wrist so tightly tears sprang into her eyes.

"Don't ever do that again," he said in a voice that was soft and deadly with unnatural calm.

"I've never hit anyone before," she said, "but, I had to stop you. You wouldn't listen to me."

His hard body betrayed that he was wild with desire, that only with the greatest effort did he manage to restrain himself.

"Maybe I was listening to what you were saying wordlessly, with your kisses, your body."

"No. I never meant . . . I don't usually act like this."

His mouth twisted cruelly. "I'd think it's a bit late for such a theatrical display of affronted honor."

Amber uttered an anguished cry and tried to tear herself away from him, but Jake caught her hands and wrenched them behind her, bending her back on the bed.

He glared at her in thundering silence.

"Jake, this is my fault as much as it's yours," she managed to say. "I know you must think I was teasing you. But I didn't lead you on deliberately. I didn't."

He gave her a long, level look that she couldn't hold. Her cheeks flooded with crimson. "Jake, please believe me," she whispered. "I guess I just felt like being close to someone and went about it in the wrong way."

To her amazement, his grip loosened, but the terrible fury in his eyes remained as he arose and strode out of the room.

Chapter Four

Amber paced the length of the sixty-foot porch with the leashed restlessness of a caged jungle cat. She scarcely felt the pain in her left ankle. She was too conscious of the man inside the house. Never had anyone affected her with such devastating power. She was anxious to get home, to feel safely in control of herself once more.

She paused, and plunged her hands deep into the pockets of her jeans. What in the name of creation was taking him so long? He'd been showering for at least half an hour.

Her gaze ran blindly over the graceful lines of Jake's immense stone ranch house, but she was still too upset by the man who owned it to admire the beauty of its simplicity. For once she didn't calculate the mansion's price tag. Nor did it occur to her to contemplate the nature of a man who wanted to live so completely alone.

Instead, she glanced anxiously at the darkening purple sky. She hadn't worn her watch, but she knew it was past seven-thirty. The party would have begun without her by now. A while ago, when she had tried to call Serena from Jake's bedroom, she hadn't been able to get a dial tone. What were Serena and Hamlin thinking?

The screen door slammed and Jake stepped outside, looking dangerously handsome in a dark suit and white dress shirt that made him look like a prosperous businessman. His black hair, still damp from his shower, gleamed. His lean brown fingers were at his throat, tightening the knot of his tie.

Her frightened eyes darted to his. His features were carefully blank. If he was still angry, he was deliberately concealing it. Oh, how she longed for the control he had over his emotions.

"Your ankle seems much better," he said in a low, quiet voice.

"Oh, it is," she replied on a slightly breathless note. "I won't be needing a doctor. Not tonight anyway."

"Sorry I took so long," he murmured.

"Oh, that's all right," she managed, struggling to get her breath back.

"I always say there's nothing like a long, cold shower to—"

She whirled, high color pouring into her cheeks. "Listen," she snapped irritably, deliberately interrupting him because she knew too well why he had needed a long, cold shower. "I need to get home at once. I tried to use the phone in your bedroom to call my brother, but it was out of order."

A half smile curved his mouth. "It's not out of order. It's only unplugged. Sometimes a phone in the bedroom can be a nuisance."

She went scarlet as his insolent eyes devoured her face and then her body. Was she only one of many women he had taken to his bedroom?

Before she could carry that mortifying thought to its conclusion, he said, "Besides, I just called Hamlin myself so he wouldn't worry about you."

"How did you know who I was?"

"Who else would Serena lend Golden to but Hamlin's sister? Whose ranch borders mine where I found you?"

"I guess it wouldn't take a genius to figure that out," she snapped waspishly.

He only laughed at her burst of temper and moved closer, so close that he towered over her and she caught the spicy scent of his after-shave. He lifted her chin with his forefinger. Jade green eyes inspected her so closely she began to tremble.

Forced to meet his gaze, Amber felt a fiery heat sweep her skin. He smiled mockingly.

"So you're Amber Johnson, the young woman every man in the county has been invited to meet tonight. Everyone, that is, except me." His voice was a slow, lazy drawl.

How should she respond to that? Try to make some joke that might distract him? Or perhaps she should be cool and cutting.

"I can't imagine that you'd care one way or the other if you were invited to meet me tonight," she managed at last.

His finger traced the sensitive skin from her jaw to her chin and back, his subtle touch a tantalizing caress that made the pulse in her neck throb beneath his fingertip.

"Oh, but I do," came the beguiling low tone that set her insides to quivering.

"I don't know what I can do about it."

"Invite me yourself," he said huskily.

"But it's Serena's party."

"It's yours too. And you owe me, in a way, after trespassing on my ranch and spying on me with your binoculars. After all, I did rescue you."

"Not from that snake!"

"So you still haven't forgiven me for that."

"As if I ever will."

"There wasn't time," he said matter-of-factly.

"Why do you want to go, anyway?"

"Maybe because I don't like being deliberately left out."

"Oh, all right," she cried. "You're invited, but only if you never mention that embarrassing episode again!"

His mouth twitched in a fleeting smile, as if her reluctance amused him. "I thought you'd never ask."

"You're not exactly Serena's favorite person, you know. Or mine either, for that matter."

"Oh, really?" He smiled boldly. "You were pretty friendly there for a while."

"That was only because... because..."

"What's happening between us can't be explained with words," he said softly.

She lifted her head to a proudly defensive angle. "Nothing's happening between us!"

"Oh, no?" he chuckled, then demanded gently, "Then why did it take thirty minutes' worth of ice water to restore my sanity? Why do we both go wild every time we touch each other?"

"Speak for yourself. I, for one, don't go wild!"

"Don't you?" he whispered, slipping his hand around her waist and drawing her against his body, so that she heard the explosive thudding of his heart. Her own sang along in answering pagan thunder.

The floor seemed to rock beneath her feet. She tipped her head back and studied his awesomely male features, struggling valiantly to appear nonchalant. That became impossible when he crushed her against the iron wall of his chest. The way he was looking at her made her feel he was making love to her in his mind. She could almost feel the caress of his hands, and she longed for him with the most primitive hunger.

"No, I don't go wild!" she said in swift denial, clinging to her air of bravado.

He only laughed. "I'll look forward to proving you wrong, little one. But don't worry." He grinned lazily. "I'm in no hurry. These things only get better the longer you wait."

Remembering Serena's warning that Jake used women and then discarded them, Amber said, "You sound very experienced."

"Let's say I'm not *in*experienced."

"You needn't bother to be so modest," she snapped.

"Usually I don't."

"And do you always get what you want, where women are concerned?" Her tortured words seemed torn from her heart.

"Not always. But this time I will."

His face was a dark mask except for his eyes, which blazed with fierce emotion every time he looked at her. Just his gaze aroused an answering response in her own body. He didn't even have to touch her. He could seduce her with his eyes. When his gaze slid to her lips, Amber had to fight the instinct to moisten them.

"One day soon, you'll come to me," he said.

"Is that a threat?" she asked weakly.

"No, love. It's a promise."

Serena flew around Amber's room, gesticulating wildly with her hands as Amber hovered over the mirror and applied a dash of eyeliner that highlighted her blue eyes and made them slant exotically.

Gone was plain Amber Johnson. In her place was a dazzling vision in flowing apricot silk. Serena, however, was so upset that she scarcely noted this startling change in her sister-in-law.

"How could you do this to me, Amber, when I warned you about Jake?"

"He did pull me up that cliff, Serena! What else could I do? He practically begged me for an invitation."

"If he crawled on his hands and knees from his ranch to mine I would have slammed the door in his face."

"I guess since he saved my life I felt I owed him something. Look, Serena, I'm sorry. I know I've ruined everything by being out so late and then dragging Jake over. But it can't be helped now. I just hope you can forgive me. I really do feel awful about it."

"Of course I forgive you," Serena said in a softer tone. "And I'm even grateful to Jake for what he did. Hamlin and I were so terrified when you didn't come back. I thought maybe Golden had thrown you. Oh, we imagined all sorts of terrible things. I guess having Jake over for a few hours won't be so bad. It just upsets me to know that he's using you to get his foot in the door over here."

"After tonight, I promise I won't see him again," Amber declared passionately.

"He won't be that easy to get rid of, let me assure you. Remember, he's got Golden, and that will give him still another excuse to come over."

Amber trembled at the thought of Jake being so determined to come over, and to cover her excitement she began to carelessly dab powder across the bridge of her nose.

After Serena left, the powder puff fell to the counter, and Amber could not stop herself from staring at her own reflection. The glamorous creature with the glowing eyes scarcely resembled the frazzled woman with thick glasses Jake Kassidy had saved on the cliff's edge. Despite her fear that someone might recognize her, she had not been able to resist wearing her contact lenses, and she could not stop herself from wondering what he would think when he saw her.

A thought gnawed at her. Was she already beginning to chase him? Was it the man, or his power to solve her problems, that so attracted her?

Never, not even at one of Don's far more glamorous affairs, had she looked lovelier. Her hair was a shower of flame against her smooth, graceful neck. At her slender throat she had dared to wear one of her own creations, an exquisite replica of a passionflower made of coral, pearls and gold.

She unbuttoned another button of her dress, but that was only to show off her necklace, not to make herself sexier for a certain brash individual who had practically invited himself to a party where he wasn't welcome. Still, as she arose to go downstairs, her blood was thrumming with the strange excitement only the thought of an encounter with that infuriating man could arouse.

When Amber came downstairs she spotted Jake immediately, though he took no notice of her. He was leaning indolently against a doorframe, a drink in one brown hand. Serena, who was almost as tall as he, was standing beside him, talking more animatedly than usual. When Jake frowned at something Serena said, Amber wondered if they were quarreling. He bent his dark head closer to Serena's, and Serena did not seem to mind this intimacy in the least.

Suddenly Amber felt deflated. She glimpsed her brother's carrot-red hair across the room, and waved to him when she caught his eye. Even when Hamlin came up to her and complimented her on her appearance as he led her to a group of men in the living room, the feeling did not go away. Through the next hour she smiled dutifully as Hamlin made introductions, but her smile felt frozen in place.

Women came up and admired her necklace. They wanted to know where they could buy one like it, and Amber was too flustered to tell them she had made it herself. Serena, who was wearing a snowflake creation Amber had given her, whispered into her ear at one point, "Amber darling, I'm telling everyone your jewelry is on sale at Sheila's in Vail."

"But you know that's a lie, Serena."

"Not for long, Amber darling."

"Sheila's is much too exclusive to handle my jewelry."

"I have a hunch Sheila will be calling you herself before the week is out."

Serena flitted away to play hostess, and Amber began to feel lonely once more. She began to drink rather more icy piña coladas than she should, and after a while she almost felt lighthearted. She was constantly surrounded by men, but none of them made her feel as alive as a certain black-haired rake could just by glancing at her. Still, she managed to joke and make light conversation in the same way she had when she'd been Don's glamorous hostess. A dozen men gazed at her with infatuated eyes.

Amber was determined to put Jake out of her mind. If he had lost interest in her the moment he had used her to get inside Serena's house, Amber was determined not to care.

Only one man, Jim Thompson, made any sort of impression on her. He was a developer who'd driven over from Steamboat Springs. He had brown hair and softly shining brown eyes in a craggy face. There was something very nice about him, and she found herself promising to go out with him the next Saturday evening. It was after she'd made this date that Jake materialized out of nowhere.

"Would you like to dance?" he asked huskily.

Her heartbeat quickened. Everything and everyone, even Jim, faded into insignificance. She was aware only of Jake as his warm, broad palm closed over hers. Never had she been more acutely conscious of the terrible weakness that made her long for the strength of a powerful man.

"My ankle . . ." she protested.

"You seem to be managing," he said, drawing her into his arms.

Her heart leaped. So he had noticed her!

"You're beautiful," he said, his green gaze sliding the length of her white throat to the place where her dress was unbuttoned above her breasts. Male eyes lingered in silent admiration. Just his gaze made her skin tingle with fire, as if he had touched her with his hands. "But I think you know how beautiful you are. Where are those thick goggles you were hiding behind this afternoon?"

"I'm wearing my contact lenses." The palms of her hands were damp with perspiration. "I was beginning to think you preferred me in glasses."

"Whatever gave you that idea?"

"You didn't look at me all night."

He chuckled. "And you missed me?"

His eyes were brilliant. A tremor of vulnerability shivered down her spine. She managed breathlessly, "Well, perhaps a little."

He hugged her tightly against his large body, a look of triumph lighting his dark features. "There, you see, I told you."

She felt his fingers brushing her long hair from her neck. The warmth of his hand slid caressingly against naked skin.

Her heart fluttered wildly as she swallowed a faint moan with a sigh. "Told me what?"

"That I would get what I wanted from you, that you would soon come to me willingly. You see, I have only to ignore you for an hour or two, and you're glad to have me back."

"Really!" she answered sharply. "You are every bit as terrible as Serena says you are!"

"I always say old friends make the worst enemies."

"That's because she knows you so well!"

"Don't forget, I know her equally well," he replied with an enigmatic smile. "I don't go around saying bad things about her."

"Maybe there's nothing you could say."

"Maybe. Or maybe she's afraid of what I could say."

"Oh."

"Forget Serena."

He pulled her closer against his body. Never had she been so feverishly aware of a man, but he was such an expert dancer that despite her excitement and her weakened ankle she followed him easily. Their bodies moved rhythmically together in flawless harmony. Though Amber scarcely knew that they did so her fingertips, resting on the black collar of his suit, found themselves caressing the soft darkness of his hair, which curled against the nape of his neck. He bent his head gently against hers, and she felt the warmth of his rough chin as it lightly grazed her smooth forehead. Again she was aware of the spicy tang of his after-shave, of the clean male scent that was his alone.

He had only to hold her, touch her, to prove his awesome power over her. The music filled the room and stirred her romantically. Or was it he alone who moved her so? Never before had she felt so vitally and yet so dangerously alive.

At last the music stopped, but when it did, though he stopped dancing, he continued to hold her in his arms long after the other dancers had left the floor.

"Looks like we're all alone," she said at last.

"I hadn't noticed." Something in his voice mesmerized her, and she forgot everything except him, and the way the heat of his body melted her against his hard, male length.

"It's amazing how one person can change everything," he said softly, almost bitterly.

"I'm not sure I know what you mean."

"Don't you?" He studied her eyes intensely. "Then you've never been in love, and you're lucky. You've never allowed someone into your life and then had them tear it to pieces. You've never had to start over, to go on after your whole world has collapsed. You've never been afraid you couldn't.''

She listened with the deepest compassion. He could have been speaking of her relationship with Don, his every word so exactly mirrored her own experiences.

"Of course, it's obvious you couldn't possibly understand," he continued. "For years I've gone through life with a chip as big as a boulder on my shoulder. Everything I've done, every success I've made, I did to prove myself as a man because one woman came so close to destroying me. I left this valley because of her, and I came back for all the wrong reasons. A long, long time ago I took a vow I would never fall in love again. A vow I've managed to keep all these years, despite a few temptations along the way.''

Did he consider her just another temptation along the way? For some reason, the thought was ridiculously painful.

"I don't understand why you're telling me this," Amber said in a small, frozen voice. "Do you warn all the women you meet?''

"I don't usually." He smiled gently, regretfully. "But there's something between us, something that I will never allow to grow into love.''

His words seemed to choke something vital and precious in her heart. She stiffened and said proudly, "Of all the arrogant, conceited things to say. As if I've been chasing after you, begging for your love.''

"Of course you haven't, but some women think desire is the same thing as love. If a man pursues them, they misconstrue his motives.''

"Well, thanks for the warning," she snapped, her voice growing even more coldly proud. "I will never misconstrue your motives...that is...if you pursue me."

His own tone softened. "Oh, I'll definitely pursue you, Amber, but I just wanted to be honest. Whatever happens between us, I don't want to hurt you. If I'm truthful now, perhaps it will lessen the possibility."

The gentle fire burning in his eyes was stirring her far more than she would have cared to admit.

"Your...nobility is very much appreciated," she said dryly. "For your own emotional safety I will confide that there are reasons...why it would be impossible for me to fall in love right now myself, even with you, my handsome Romeo. I, too, would never want to lead you on and have you misconstrue my feelings as anything other than what they are. The very last thing I want is to become seriously involved with a man."

"So you've been hurt, too?" he said softly.

"Destroyed," she murmured.

"I didn't think life had left you untouched. There's something in your eyes."

She bit her lips and jerked her gaze from his face. He saw too much.

"I see now why you were making such a deliberate effort to be unattractive with those awful glasses. You want nothing more to do with men."

She nodded, because there was safety in his thinking that was her only reason.

The music resumed. This time it was a slow, smoky blend of saxophones and muted trumpets that filled every fiber of Amber's being with a deep, yearning sensuousness, mocking her fierce determination to be indifferent to this man. Once more Jake folded her against his body, and the minute they began to move together she was aware of the rigid tension flowing from his muscles.

"I've been so lonely," he said, his breath a warm caress against her ear. "For so long."

"So have I," she confessed. "Oh, so have I." Why was it that being in his arms made her so profoundly aware of that fact?

When the music stopped again, neither of them noticed. He had bent his lips and taken hers ever so gently, deliberately attempting to control his passion.

Just as the kiss began to deepen, and she felt her body quickening with wildfire need, he released her mouth. Slowly Amber came back to consciousness and opened her eyes. Amber grew aware of Serena watching them from across the room, a look of pain marring the soft, dark beauty of her face.

Serena tore her eyes away from them and fled the room as if deeply upset. Amber looked toward Jake in puzzlement, and saw that he, too, had seen Serena's reaction to their kiss.

"I don't understand why she's so set against you," Amber whispered, depressed that her new friendship upset Serena.

Jake seemed suddenly to be possessed by some intense emotion as dark and threatening as Serena's. A suspicion about Serena and Jake was beginning to form in the depths of Amber's mind.

"There's no need for you to understand," he replied swiftly. "Let's get out of here. More than anything, I want to be alone with you."

He wore the look of a man who wanted to run away

from some terrible pain that was still too unbearable to face. How well Amber understood such feelings.

In answer, she gripped his hand more tightly in her own, and allowed him to pull her quickly toward the door.

Chapter Five

Jake drove in silence, choosing ranch roads that wound high into the mountains. In twenty minutes they had met the flaring headlights of only one car. Never had Amber felt so alone with any man. It was as if the ink-black night had swallowed them, and they were the only man and the only woman left on earth.

She had had this feeling more than once when she was with Jake. When they were together, he made everything else, even her troubles with Don, seem insignificant. She felt alive again, young, as if she could start over. She felt filled with anticipation. The world seemed more sharply colored, yet more dangerous.

His mere presence could make her blood fire with excitement even when she fought to subdue her treacherous responses. She wanted to hate him because his power over her forced her to see that her old weakness had not been defeated. She wanted to dislike him for the way she lost control when she was around him. She wanted to hate him for his own superb control. She wanted to hate him especially for the arrogant words of warning he had given her at the party. He had made it clear his intention was to seduce her and yet remain emotionally uninvolved with her. He was determined to possess her so he could stamp out his need of her.

He had justified Serena's earlier, bitter words: "Amber, darling...he'd use you and discard you."

That was the last sort of experience any intelligent woman would deliberately seek, and yet, despite everything, Amber was passionately drawn to him.

Jake had not spoken since they had left the party, but she was keenly aware that he was still gripped by whatever powerful emotion had driven him from the room.

So she had been right after all when she had thought he was chased by demons as fierce as her own. Strangely, though this frightened her and made him seem even more dangerous, he was all the more attractive to her. She wanted to help him, to reach out to him, even though some instinct warned her not to.

The pavement ended, and the tires bit into gravel as the road, which had once been an old railroad bed, narrowed and wound higher up the mountain. In places it was little more than a path carved beneath thick fir and spruce. Slowly the dense forest thinned, and they climbed above the treeline.

In the moonlight, Amber could see stumps gleaming like tombstones in the great flat open space between the jagged slopes, where trees had been cut nearly a hundred years ago to build the railroad. Only a few stunted specimens had grown back, and they hugged the bare rocks, their branches shaking as a fierce wind gusted through the mountain pass.

Jake turned the truck off the main road onto an even narrower one, so deeply rutted it was almost impassable. He came to a stop in front of a ruined cabin, grabbed a blanket from behind the seat and reached past Amber to open her door.

Through thin apricot silk she felt his muscled arm brushing against the pointed tips of her breasts. She gave a little gasp, but he seemed not to notice that she had begun to tremble. He opened his own door and came around to help her out, his strong, warm fingers curling around her tiny hand. His other arm reached for her waist, and Amber felt her body arch pliantly into his sinewy length as she slid against him.

He held her tightly, a molten sensuality binding their bodies. She struggled to find the will to push him away.

"Do you always help girls out of your truck and then hold them this way?" she asked, a little breathlessly.

He did not release her. "Only you." His voice was low and controlled.

Amber was glad of the chill mountain breeze that cooled her heated skin. Though it was a summer evening and she felt hot, the air itself was cold. Amber lost her battle to resist him, and Jake's arms remained protectively about her, his warmth and nearness making her all the more feverishly conscious of him.

He led her toward the tumbledown cabin. "This used to be an old railroad station, but it hasn't been used since the thirties."

"Why did you bring me here?"

"You always want to know exactly what's going on, don't you, little one?" Amber caught the hint of laughter in his deep voice.

"It might be dangerous not to, with you. I was just curious as to your intentions," she said primly.

"Whether they're honorable or dishonorable?" He smiled mockingly. The bold heat of his gaze seared her as disturbingly as his body had only moments before.

"Well?" she whispered.

"Hopefully they're..." He seemed to hesitate on the word "honorable," and she held her breath until he expelled the three syllables most regretfully. Then he amended, "For the moment."

"That doesn't sound too reassuring."

"I'm a man of many weaknesses and you, apparently, are one of them."

Their glances met.

She was filled with tempestuous excitement. In his eyes she saw intense emotion.

He continued, "This is one of my favorite places. I used to come here as a kid to dig up hundred-year-old railway spikes. They sell them in the ski resorts for five dollars apiece."

"And did you find any?" Was she asking only because this topic was safer than the one before? Or was it that she wanted to know everything about him, even his boyhood amusements?

"Loads of them. Each one was a treasure, though. Sometimes the earth was packed so hard it might take me an hour just to dig one up. Sometimes when the road had been freshly graded you could pick them up by the pound in the ditches."

Moonlight had turned the mountains to silver and slanting purple blackness. She found herself concentrating on the way the shadows intensified the carved planes of his rugged face, the way the pale light gleamed in the ebony thickness of his hair.

"It's beautiful up here," Amber said, deliberately attempting to distract herself from those compelling male features. "And it smells good, too." She inhaled the brisk sweetness of the night air. "The stars seem brighter, the sky blacker."

"It's even nicer in the daytime. You feel like you can see forever. There's always snow in the highest mountains, and there are the wild flowers. I always feel free up here."

His arms tightened around Amber's waist, drawing her more completely against himself. She began to shiver under the pressure of his hands. She felt the wildness in him surging to the surface. She was aware of a languid dissolving sensation within herself.

His lips came down to claim hers in a quick sure kiss. She half-opened her mouth and bent her head back. He explored every curve of her voluptuously lush soft lips. Then his tongue went inside and tasted the sweetness of her. His hand moved to the side of her neck, his thumb resting against the racing pulse there. Her arms lifted around his shoulders, her fingertips brushing the soft hair on his neck. She was quivering like a frightened animal. When he lifted his mouth, his grave eyes studying the gentle beauty of her upturned face, she was sure he could read her chaotic emotions all too easily.

The hot imprint of his mouth burned her lips; the clean scent of him filled her nostrils. The taste of him remained. Her heart was pounding irregularly.

He locked his hands together at the small of her back and pulled her more firmly against him. Amber's own fingers were spread against his shirt in mute protest, even though she really wanted him to hold her. All she could think of was how strong the solidness of his chest felt, how her mouth still tingled, how her body melted so naturally into his and how even his gentlest kiss inflamed her.

"We shouldn't," she whispered, struggling weakly against him.

"Oh, but we should." His eyes looked deeply into hers, crinkling at the corners, taking note of her confusion. "You have no idea what a godsend you are, Amber," he murmured.

He pulled her inside the partially ruined house. There was no ceiling except the moon and the stars and the spray of the Milky Way, but the walls shielded them from the cold wind. Amber could hear the murmur from the forest beneath as the wind sighed among the spruce and pines. There was the faint sound of one distant scraggly aspen, its dry leaves rustling.

"I like your necklace," he said softly. He fingered the delicate coral petals, and even this gentlest grazing of his fingertips against her throat languorously teased her senses.

She breathed deeply, trying to gain some semblance of composure. "Thank you. I made it. It's supposed to be a passionflower."

"An appropriate ornament for the lady who's wearing it," he said, his voice warm and caressing.

"I'm not sure."

"I'm very sure." His tone had gone low with sexual innuendo. "You're obviously a woman of many talents."

"I'm trying to make my living designing jewelry. I've only just begun to sell my work. Soon, perhaps, I'll be able to afford my own apartment."

"You sound very fierce. It must be terribly important to you, then, to become independent."

She nodded. "All my life I've let someone else take care of me. It's time I grew up."

His hot gaze ran downward from the loveliness of her softly glowing face to where her breasts heaved against gauzy silk. "You look all grown up to me."

His bold eyes lingered until she blushed.

"That's not what I meant!"

"You're saying you're not looking for a man to take care of you."

"That's right." Why did her voice sound so defensive?

"As I said before, you're a very unusual woman. Most women are dying to have a man shoulder their problems."

Guilt made her wince. "I suppose women are always chasing you."

She was aware of an odd pang of jealousy that was even stronger than her guilt.

"When I'm chased, I usually run," he said matter-of-factly. "Male instinct. I like to do the chasing."

She was acutely conscious of his searing eyes upon her once more. He laid the blanket on the ground.

Amber glanced down at it, then into his dark face. She was remembering the fire of his kiss, the predatory gleam in his eyes. "I shouldn't have let you bring me here."

"Why not?"

"We're so alone."

"You preferred the party?" he asked in a low voice.

"No," she admitted. "Though now it seems safer."

"My first impression was that you were a girl who liked to live dangerously," he continued softly. "Perhaps that's what made you so interesting this afternoon, even when you were sporting your glasses and that prim little bun. There you were, spying on me, then pretending to be Serena. When I found you grappling with that rattler while you hung to the side of that cliff, I thought: Here is a girl unlike any I've ever known.''

She was ridiculously pleased at the sound of amusement and approval in his voice. ''First impressions are usually wrong,'' she said, a note of asperity in her voice.

He smiled. ''Are they? Then I'll have to give that tried-and-true gem more thought.''

''And, of course,'' she said piously, ''there are many kinds of danger. Some far preferable to others.''

''Are you saying you prefer the dangers of snakes and cliffs to the dangers of men?''

She gave a quick, nervous laugh and glanced away.

''Of *me*?'' he persisted. Laughter danced in his vivid green eyes.

''Perhaps.''

''Do you want to go back to the party, then?''

She merely looked at him.

''You have only to say the word,'' he said with grave gentleness.

''Why did you bring me here?''

''Because I wanted to be alone with you. And this place is special to me.''

''It's very remote.''

He lay down and drew her onto the blanket beside him. ''Maybe that's why I like it.''

She was trembling from his touch, from the voice that wrapped her in velvet and made her forget all the carefully learned wisdom she had no intention of forgetting.

''That's what scares me,'' she said shakily. There was something about lying down beside him beneath magic starlight that was powerfully erotic.

''You don't have to be afraid. I won't do anything you don't want me to.''

"That doesn't entirely reassure me."

"Then you admit you do go wild when I touch you."

"I admit . . . that you affect me."

"You affect me too." Something low and vitally passionate had come into his voice.

For a time they lay in silence. Amber was so intensely aware of him she could hardly breathe.

"There's so much about you I don't understand," she said, thinking safety lay in conversation. "You grew up here, and yet you left for many years."

"There was nothing for me here, so I moved on."

His tenseness had returned. Her sideways glance observed him gazing out the ruined windows at the mountains and the moonlight, a thoughtful expression on his ruggedly carved features. The suggestion of grimness around his mouth made her want to reach out with her fingertips and gently smooth it away.

"You were poor?" she asked softly.

"I wasn't referring to money. But, yes, I had no money."

"So you went away to seek your fortune."

Again he looked at her. His green eyes were midnight-dark, shimmering and mysterious. They seemed fathomless to Amber, and she was disconcerted as he focused their steadfast attention on her face.

There was pain in his past, just as there was pain in hers. There was no room in his life for a new woman. It was a warning she should not ignore.

"You could say that I left to seek my fortune, I suppose," he was saying.

"You must have made a lot of money." Why did that inner demon always drive her to pursue the topic of money?

"Yes."

"Then you came back, as abruptly as you left." She was aware of him watching her intently, and she forced herself to stare beyond him toward the mountains.

"I always meant to come back." His fingers caught her chin and turned her head toward his searching gaze. "This is my home. No matter where I went, I could never forget it. You can run away from everything but yourself. Eventually there comes a day when you wake up and think: Today is the day I stop running." Something fierce and terrible came into his voice, something that contained the memory of some awesome passion he could not entirely conceal. "One morning I said, Today is the day I go after what I really want."

He stared at her, his expression one of savage pain. His suffering drew her to him and made her feel profoundly compassionate. He kept looking at her, saying nothing, his eyes alone speaking to hers. And he seemed to find some solace in the discovery that she yearned to ease his pain, because he smiled faintly.

Amber made no effort to twist away from his fingers, though she knew she should. He saw too much. Her vulnerability to him was too easily read. His touch made her feel she belonged to him, and she was determined never again to belong to any man. Besides, he had made it clear he could never care for her in any real way.

"So you woke up one day, just like that?" she tossed off, trying to sound indifferent and thereby lighten the intensity of his dark mood.

"Just like that," he echoed softly, mockingly, his passion once again suppressed. Jake let his hand slide from her chin to her shoulder.

"Was it the right thing, your coming back here?"

"Oh, definitely." She felt his fingers tighten in gentle possession.

"Aren't the demons that haunted you still here?"

"They're here, but they seem to be losing their power."

"Then you're free now."

A furrow creased his brow. "Not exactly. I think I've stumbled onto a new demon."

"What do you mean?"

"There's you," he whispered.

Her heart began to beat wildly. "You said at the party—"

"Forget everything I said at the party."

"Didn't you mean what you said?"

"Then I did. Or at least I wanted to."

"Let's see if I have it right," she pressed, determined to taunt him. "I'm to be nothing more than another 'temptation along the way.'"

"You're certainly a temptation."

She wanted to be so much more. All her aching need was in her face. Her eyes were luminous. He saw her passion, and he misunderstood.

"I want to make love to you. I can't seem to help myself where you're concerned." His voice rang with the same uncontrollable intensity that she had heard only moments before.

"That's why you brought me here, to make love to me, isn't it?" she murmured.

His gaze searched her frightened face with unnerving thoroughness. "You want me to, don't you, little one? Despite your virtuous determination not to?" He twined his fingers in the silken waves of her perfumed hair. "I knew it the first time I held you in my arms."

Amber's pulse hammered chaotically. A heady intoxication overpowered her senses. "No." The whispered word was inaudible. "No, I don't."

"You're not a very good liar." One corner of his mouth curved into an enchanting crooked smile.

His dark, virile appeal wove a spell. It took all her willpower to make even a feeble show of resistance, so powerfully did he attract her.

Shaking, she sat up and buried her face in her hands. She found him dangerously compelling, and he knew it. He had admitted his loneliness. He probably saw her as an easily available woman, and he wanted to use her for a temporary lover to satisfy his physical needs.

She blindly gazed down at him. His roughly sculpted face was set in implacable lines, cast half in shadow by the silvery moonlight streaming over him. The rich velvet shades of his hair gleamed. His eyes were brilliant with dark unquenchable desire.

A wave of terrible longing washed over Amber, but she was determined to deny it.

"Take me home, Jake," she said shakily. "Now. Before—"

"Not before I make love to you."

"No."

She tried to bolt from him, but he grabbed her, lowering her beneath his body.

"I've wanted you since the moment I saw you, rattlesnake, thick glasses and all."

Amber made a strangled attempt to protest. She began to kick, her slim legs flailing helplessly. Her fists pounded at his broad shoulders and chest, but he was too strong.

With his legs locked around her waist, he unfastened his tie. She watched in horror as he shrugged off his coat. Then came his shirt. Her stomach knotted at the sight of his bronzed, muscled shoulders and belly, powerful and sinuously firm. With the shedding of his clothes, it seemed he had relinquished whatever thin veneer of civilization separated man from beast.

He reached for his belt buckle. She gave a little shriek and tried to roll away from him. His hand whipped out to grip her arm and drag her back. He lowered his body once more onto the rumpled wool blanket, half-covering hers.

The crushing weight of his chest pressed her breasts against rigid naked muscle. She felt the heat of him burning through thin apricot silk. Her dress had come up, twisting itself around her hips, exposing her legs. Doubtless, soon his large hands would shred the flimsy silk.

Her hands strained futilely against his arms. She twisted her head to avoid his mouth, but she couldn't stop him from exploring her throat with tantalizingly soft kisses.

His insolent lips moved further down. She felt their bruising heat from the sensitive skin of her bare shoulders to the satin-smooth hollow between her breasts. He cupped the full ripe globes, teasing and warming each soft nipple until it peaked in ardent betrayal. Everything he did aroused her. His burning kisses sent the world spinning, and she felt herself drawn into the vortex of his desire.

His rough palm stroked her cheek tenderly before he caught her chin to still her head from twisting so frantically. His dark face bent over hers, taking her lips with arrogant mastery, pressing his tongue deeply into her mouth. His hands ruffled the tangled waves of her silken hair. She wanted nothing more than to give in to the splendor of his touch.

She was aware of his weight, of his long legs against her own, his thighs like iron. It was no use to fight him. He was too strong, too knowledgeable about women. He felt the wildness of her response. He knew that she wanted him as desperately as he wanted her, just as he knew how dangerously near she hovered to the abyss of complete surrender.

His mouth devoured the gentle softness of her lips. He kissed her hungrily until, against her will, her lips moved against his, tentatively at first, then more passionately.

She managed one last show of defiance. "You don't know what you're doing," she whispered between breathless kisses.

"Maybe not," he agreed in a throaty growl that caressed her lips. "But I'm sure as hell enjoying it."

She clung to him, aching for him, wanting him. His kisses grew harder, and they made that insidious flame inside her flare even higher. She moaned in desperation.

Jake chuckled softly. "And you're enjoying it too, little one."

What did that matter when their reasons for making love were so wrong?

He was running away from something in his past. All he wanted was something quick and easy. She was running too, looking for something he would never be willing to give her.

"Oh, Jake, no... Please, don't," she begged in agonized protest, trying not to be overwhelmed by the drugging effect of more addictive kisses.

"Amber, stop fighting it," he muttered thickly. "You know you want me."

"Yes! I do! But I've asked you to let me go! If you take me now, it will be against my will!"

"Against..." Jake froze, and something inside Amber froze, too, as he wrenched himself away from her. She watched as he raked his hand through his thick black hair. When he looked at her, his eyes were brilliant and hard.

"Damn you, Amber," he whispered, his voice filled with pain.

She reached for him, and when she touched him, he began to tremble.

He tore his arm away from the comfort of her gentle caress. "Get away!" he growled. "Don't you understand? Go quickly before..."

Before he lost what little control he had.

She got up, sick with shame and the pain of his rejection. She stepped outside, and the cold air whipped her skin as she ran stumbling toward the truck. With clumsy fingers she started the ignition and backed down the rutted path toward the road.

She was vaguely aware of Jake shouting her name as he ran out of the cabin and down the path after her.

"Amber! Stop! We're thirty miles from nowhere."

He deserved to walk! To hell and back! She didn't care if it took him all night! She pressed down hard on the accelerator, and the truck shot forward in a burst of speed, only to jounce heavily into a deep hole. There was a terrible clanking underneath the truck, as though something metallic had ruptured.

"What the devil are you doing to my truck, woman?" came an infuriated male shout.

The rest of his words were drowned by the noise of the tires spinning in gravel. Jake had almost reached Amber before she managed to get the truck out of the rut and gun it toward the main road. She drove a quarter of a mile at breakneck speed, rocks flying and thick clouds of choking dust rising behind her, before she applied the brakes and slowed the truck.

He was the most maddening man she'd ever known! She should leave him! She should!

She killed the motor and collapsed upon the steering wheel.

She must have sat slumped over the wheel for at least ten minutes before the sound of a man's heavy tread on the thickly packed gravel road startled her into consciousness. She paled when she saw Jake striding toward her, his coat slung over his wide shoulders as if he were indifferent to the cold that would have had her shivering helplessly.

He opened her door and said quietly, "Thank you for waiting, Amber."

She stared bleakly into his hard eyes. "I...I couldn't leave you."

She slid wordlessly to the other side of the cab, and he got in. They drove back to the ranch in strangled silence. When they reached Hamlin's house, she tried in vain to smooth her dress and her hair. He watched her futile efforts grimly.

"I—I don't guess I'll be seeing you again," she said. "Jake, I'm sorry."

He cut her off. "Don't apologize."

"I just wanted to say that I know that what happened tonight was partly my fault."

"That again." He groaned wearily. "It doesn't matter, Amber."

"But it does."

"Look, we're just different. That's all. Kisses and embraces and sweet promises that mean nothing aren't enough for me."

"No," she lashed out at him, her anger and hurt getting the better of her judgment. "You're after quick sex. You just want to use me and discard me."

He grabbed her wrist and pulled her closer. "Use you and discard you? Is that your idea of what our making love would be? What makes you think like that?"

"Serena says that's all you ever do with your women!" Amber cried.

"Serena should keep her damn mouth shut! She's a fine one to talk about using people and discarding them."

"What's that supposed to mean?"

"Let Serena tell you, since it's obvious I'm such a favorite topic of gossip between the two of you."

"Scarcely our favorite, I assure you. But I should have listened to her, Jake. She warned me to avoid you."

"I'll just bet she did." His teeth gleamed white against his swarthy skin, his grim smile giving him the look of a pirate. "A pity you didn't listen to her. But then, it's always difficult to appreciate the value of good advice until it's too late."

"On that note," she snapped, "I'll say good night. Make it goodbye. That's more permanent."

"Hopefully," he added, his deep voice as biting as her own.

She began to struggle with the door, but couldn't manage the handle because she was trembling so violently.

He reached across her, his hateful, sardonic smile broadening. "Allow me," he murmured with mock gallantry, "to help you fling yourself out of my life. I'm as impatient for that blissful state as you."

He unlatched the door effortlessly, and she flew outside, almost tumbling headfirst from the truck, so anxious was she to escape him.

"Careful, little one," he warned. "Save some of that fire for the next man who wants to do more than let you get your kicks from watching him with your binoculars.

"You don't ever intend to forget that, do you?"

"Never. I will cherish that memory until my dying day!"

"As far as I'm concerned, that's one day that can't come a minute too soon!"

"It's always nice to know one's friends have something to look forward to."

"Jake Kassidy, you will never be my friend!"

"I never wanted to be. I've always had something much more interesting in mind for the two of us."

"I can't imagine what that might be."

"Come over any time. I'll be glad to satisfy your curiosity."

"Why do you so enjoy wallowing in the gutter? Can't you ever think of anything besides sex?"

"Not when I'm around you."

"Oh, so now you're blaming me for your depraved character?"

"In a way you're responsible."

"Of all the unmitigated gall! You're a snake, Jake Kassidy, with vile, loathsome instincts, and I never want to see you again."

"And I thought you were a girl with a fondness for snakes."

She shot him a killing look and slammed the door. "If there were a cliff, I would kick you off it."

"And you said *I* was the one with vile, loathsome instincts," came his silken rejoinder. "Sounds to me like we have a lot more in common than you care to admit."

She ran furiously up the walk. The last thing she heard was the sound of his cynical laughter.

Chapter Six

Amber had no wish to talk about Jake with Serena and Hamlin, so she was glad they had already left for Denver when she came downstairs the morning after her experience with Jake. They'd invited her to go with them but she'd declined, saying she needed to work. Amber spent the rest of the day alone, working. And thinking about Jake Kassidy.

Breakfast Monday morning proved to be the ordeal she'd feared.

"So, how was your date with Jake?" Serena demanded after an awkward ten-minute silence. There was a strange edge to her voice. She jabbed her cigarette into a crystal ashtray, but for once Amber was too upset herself to be concerned about Serena's nervousness.

Amber was carefully lashing a lump of scrambled egg into jagged bits with her fork. "Jake Kassidy is insufferable, and I never want to see him again," she said, without glancing at her sister-in-law.

Hamlin looked up from his newspaper and smiled mildly. "My! My! Such violence, little sister, and at breakfast. Just look at your poor egg. You know what they say—hate and love are very closely related."

"Not in this case, brother dear," Amber muttered, dropping her fork with a clatter. "Go back to your paper."

"It does seem safer." Hamlin picked up the classified section and slumped behind it.

Amber had the impression that behind his paper, her brother's ears were pricked as high as a jackrabbit's on either side of that thatch of unruly red hair.

"I certainly hope Jake feels the same way about you, Amber darling," Serena interjected. "If he doesn't, you haven't seen the last of him. Jake can be very persistent when he wants something."

"How well I know! Believe me, you were right. He was only after sex. He never wants to see me again."

Hamlin's bright eyes peered over his paper. "Does that mean he got some? Or that he didn't?"

"Shut up, brother dear!"

"I hate to say 'I told you so,' Amber darling," Serena said smugly, sipping her coffee, her nervousness apparently gone.

Amber resisted the temptation to pick up her fork and instead began toying with her toast. She was troubled. Not at all her usual self. Her lacerated egg had grown cold. The thought of eating that pale rubbery substance made her positively nauseous. She hadn't even drunk her coffee. She was usually starving in the morning, but today, after a sleepless night of thinking about Jake and their impossible relationship, she wasn't hungry at all.

How was it that he had the power to disturb her even when she had passionately resolved never to see him again? She was in a rage to take out her frustration on someone. Serena's words kept echoing in the back of her mind in singsong fashion.

I hate to say I told you so. I hate to say I told you so. I hate . . .

"No, you don't, Serena," Amber cried aloud, retaliating against the silent taunting voice. "You love every minute of telling me 'I told you so.'"

"I do not! And you shouldn't snap at me." Serena got up and began to stack the breakfast dishes. "Jake's the one you're mad at."

"You're so right," Amber admitted in a gentler tone. "Sorry, Serena. It's just that Saturday night left me in a terrible mood."

"I can imagine. Jake can be pretty impossible. You're much better off now that you're determined to have nothing more to do with him."

"Sure," Amber muttered.

Funny, but she didn't feel better off. It was awful, but the more passionately she denounced Jake, the worse she was beginning to feel. Suddenly it seemed that the walls of the breakfast room were closing in on her, and that Serena and Hamlin were oppressive companions. Amber wanted nothing so much as the dubious pleasure of being allowed to wallow in her misery alone, without having to contend with their interfering opinions.

"Well, I think I'd better go out to the shop and get to work, Serena, before I go crazy thinking about what a fool I was to have had anything to do with him," Amber said briskly.

Hamlin replaced the classified section on the table. His blue eyes brightened when they fell upon his younger sister. He wore the look of a man ready to leap into battle.

"Frankly, girls, nothing you two have said has made a lick of sense. Amber, you're acting like a fool. What's wrong with a man wanting sex, I'd like to know? I'd be more worried if he didn't. It's a perfectly natural inclination. Or so I was always told."

Amber stared at Hamlin as if he'd sprouted horns. "Traitor," she growled.

"Jake's a healthy male animal," Hamlin defended.

"You've certainly got that right! He's all animal!"

Hamlin merely smiled benignly in that infuriatingly superior big-brother way of his, as he rose and put his arms around his wife. "I'm surprised at you, Amber. Sex is the basis of any successful man-woman relationship. Like mine with Serena." He buried his lips in Serena's glossy black curls. "Isn't it, darling?" Serena managed to nod bleakly.

"I hardly need a lecture on the merits of marital sex, brother dear. You may remember, I was married once myself."

"But perhaps not so blissfully as Serena and I."

He leaned down to kiss Serena once more, but Serena turned her face away. "Won't you be late, Hamlin darling, if you don't hurry?" came the sound of her choked voice.

Hamlin couldn't see his wife's eyes, but Amber saw them. They were glazed with guilt and pain.

Hamlin merely pressed his wife's hand. "There, darling. What would I do without you to remember things for me?"

The phone began to ring, and Amber flew into the kitchen to answer it, glad of the opportunity to escape Hamlin and his obnoxious advice as well as her growing suspicions concerning Serena's strange unhappiness.

A man's deep voice said, "Hello, Amber."

"Jake," Amber whispered, in a tiny, hope-filled voice she instantly despised.

"This is Jim Thompson."

"Oh."

"You remember me from the party?"

"Of course." She tried to sound thrilled as she murmured, "I'm so glad you called."

"I was wondering if you'd mind changing our plans for next Saturday night to tonight? We could drive into Steamboat Springs for dinner."

"That's fine, Jim. I'd love to."

"Hope you like Italian food, because there's a great restaurant I know."

"I love Italian food."

They talked a few minutes longer, but their conversation did little to cheer Amber. Despite her firm desire not to think of Jake Kassidy, he constantly intruded. She had wanted it to be him on the phone, and she was almost angry at Jim because he wasn't Jake. Of course, she told herself, that was only because Jake had had the last word Saturday night, and she wanted to have the satisfaction of telling him off more satisfactorily.

Later, when she went out to the shop to sketch designs, she couldn't get anything accomplished. None of her ideas seemed to work. Her designs were flat and uninteresting. She tore one after another into pieces, until the concrete floor looked as untidy as a hamster's cage. She felt as unproductive as a hamster spinning its wheel. Finally she worked on one gold ring that she'd enjoyed creating a few days before. It was a frog, of modern design with tiny jade eyes, but she hated it once she'd finished it. She kept wondering why had she given it those green eyes. Why not red? Blue? Anything but green!

From time to time while she worked the telephone in the shop rang, and every time it did, her heart jerked expectantly. Once she almost picked it up, despising herself for the weakness in her that wanted the black-haired devil who lived on the next ranch to call.

After the casually arrogant way Jake had treated her, why did she still long to hear from him? Every time the phone rang, she had to fight anew her temptation to pick it up until Serena answered it in the house.

Later that afternoon, while Amber was getting ready for her date with Jim, Serena came into her bedroom. Serena was smoking, and she seemed more agitated than usual. Her face was deathly pale, her painted lips slashes of vivid scarlet against her white skin.

Serena forced a smile and said, "I have good news and bad news, Amber darling. First the good news: I talked to Sheila, and she wants to see everything you've got."

"You're kidding!" Amber grabbed Serena and hugged her. "Did she call? Or did you call her?"

"I called her, but she said she'd been inundated with calls all morning asking if she had anything you'd done."

"Serena, I'm not sure I'm good enough."

"Nonsense. Tomorrow I'm going to drive you to Vail. And I don't want you downgrading yourself in front of Sheila. She's got the instincts of a shark, and if she thinks she can drive a hard bargain, she will. I'm going along to make sure she doesn't."

"You sound so confident."

"You're good, Amber darling. Soon everyone will know it. Maybe if you hear it from someone like Sheila, you'll start believing it yourself."

Amber looked doubtful.

"And now for the bad news." Serena's face lost its animation, and went white once more. "Jake called you five times. He left this number where he could be reached." She placed a crumpled scrap of paper on Amber's dresser.

Amber grabbed it and tore it into tiny pieces. "I'm not interested in anything he might have to say."

Serena was watching her. "I certainly hope not, Amber darling. I don't want to see you hurt."

Amber turned away, feeling uncomfortable. Was that Serena's real reason? Or was she in love with Jake herself?

"You should be glad, then, that I'm going out with Jim tonight," Amber managed at last.

"Oh, I am. He's just the gentle sort of man a girl like you needs."

For some reason, Serena's statement grated on Amber's nerves. The minute Serena left, Amber jumped up and grabbed the waste can.

What had Serena meant? That Amber was so dull she could never keep a man like Jake? Amber rifled the contents of the can, reverently retrieving each jagged piece of the note.

Bit by tattered bit she reconstructed the telephone number. Then she stared at it in a state of heart-thumping paralysis.

Jake had called five times. That he had done so meant more than anything. Yet because it meant so much, her feelings of hurt intensified.

She lifted the phone and held it against her, her fingers hovering above the dial. She wanted to apologize. She wanted to tell him about Sheila. She set the receiver down again.

There was no way she could return his calls—even though she wanted to. She was too afraid, and much too stubbornly proud to let him think she might care about him.

Her anger was gone. All she felt was pain and the most terrible confusion. She thought of the way she was treating Serena and Hamlin. It was ridiculous of her to keep getting mad at them when it was Jake who was driving her crazy.

What in the world was happening to her?

That evening, Amber made herself especially beautiful for her date with Jim. She wore her most alluring dress, a feminine, gauzy, flowered thing that clung to her as revealingly as a ballerina's gossamer costume. Her flame-colored hair fell softly against her pale face. Her long-lashed eyes were darkened with brown liner so that they were as provocative as those of an Egyptian temptress.

It was important that no one think her heart wasn't in this date with Jim. Under no circumstances did she want Serena and Hamlin to guess how miserable she really was.

Amber was so anxious to escape the house, that she was downstairs waiting in the living room thirty minutes before Jim was to arrive. She had scarcely sat on Serena's brocade couch five minutes, when she heard a car outside.

She ran to the window. A familiar blue truck with a white horse trailer was parked at the gate. A tall man whose bold handsomeness was achingly familiar came around from the driver's side of the truck and opened the gate.

Jake! Her fingers flew to her mouth as she watched him stride up the walk toward the house. Her heart seemed to stop beating, and then began to thump at a frightening pace.

His knock resounded upon the front door. It was Paula's day off, and Serena and Hamlin were upstairs watching television in their bedroom.

Hesitantly Amber went to the door. She took a deep breath and then threw it open.

His green eyes swept her from the top of her apricot head to the shiny tips of her patent-leather toes. With an intensity that alarmed her, they returned to gaze on the blossom that swelled above one heaving bosom.

She went hot all over, and inhaled a fortifying gulp of air.

"Look me in the eye, damn you," she demanded. "I'm a person, not just a body for your male perusal."

His slow smile was devastating. His mocking eyes rose slowly to her face, and a quiver darted through her.

"Oh, really?" came the deep masculine tones that made her go boneless.

"Yes."

"That dress invites my...er...now what was that quaint turn of phrase you just used so charmingly?" A taunting element had come into his voice. "It seems to have slipped my mind."

The devil! Not for a minute did she believe he had forgotten what she'd said. Especially not with that smirk of his.

"Male perusal," she snapped, longing to claw his dark skin until his eyes gleamed with pain instead of that bright insolence.

His smile broadened. "Ah yes. Male perusal. Do you stay awake nights dreaming up those gems?"

Black patent toes shifted nervously. "I assume the reason we're both standing out here is that you wanted to talk to me."

He nodded.

"Then say what you have to say."

"I'm getting around to it."

"You seem determined to take the long route."

An odd look came into his eyes. "Look, this isn't any easier for me than it is for you. I saw you at the window, Amber. You didn't look too happy when you realized it was me. I'm surprised you even had the guts to answer the door."

"Why wouldn't I?" she retorted coolly. "I'm not afraid of you." Why was she trembling so violently, then? Why did her heart flutter so chaotically?

"You certainly weren't answering your phone this afternoon."

"I had work to do."

"So much that you couldn't return your calls?"

"I saw no reason to."

"Serena gave you my message, then?"

"Yes."

Amber turned away, but he gripped her arm and pulled her back, holding her so close against him she could savor the warmth and feel and scent of him.

"And you weren't even a little bit curious as to why I was calling?" he muttered in a hoarse rasp that somehow suggested pain.

"No." Amber choked back a sob. "After Saturday night I didn't want to have anything more to do with you."

His face went as bloodless as if she'd struck him; his green eyes turned to stone. Something in his proud expression tore at her heart.

She felt his muscles go rigid before he released her. The bruised places on her arms throbbed where his fingers had held her, yet she longed to have his hands upon her body again.

She had hurt him, and even though she had wanted desperately to do so, having succeeded, she found no satisfaction. There was only a terrible, dead, aching place in her own heart.

"Well, I can't say I blame you for not wanting to see me or talk to me again," he said in a low tone that spoke of agony.

He lowered his black head as if he couldn't bear to face her. She should have turned on her heel and retreated to safety now that the fight had gone out of him, but something more powerful than pride held her.

She stared at him in bleak confusion. Then the deep yearning she felt for him pushed everything else aside.

Gently she said, "Jake, I—I did want to see you." She reached out and touched his arm. "Too much, I think."

He didn't look at her, but he didn't pull his hand away, either.

"Jake," she begged, "you could at least look at me." She pulled at his arm, forcing him to face her.

"It's not so easy. I feel like hell for the way I treated you," he muttered. His eyes were dark and savage with some intense, shuttered emotion.

"If that's an apology," she whispered, "I—"

"It is. Not that I expect you to forgive me."

"But I do."

"How could you? I was such a complete bastard. I don't know if I've ever wanted a woman as much as I wanted you the other night, Amber, but that was no excuse for the way I treated you. I just went after you without stopping to consider that your feelings were quite different from mine. I'm sorry for that. I've brought Golden back so you won't have to come after her and risk seeing me again."

"Jake, I—I do forgive you. And as I said before, I don't blame you entirely for what happened. It was a provocative thing I did, watching you with those binoculars, then behaving the way I did in your bedroom. I gave you the wrong idea about myself. I don't usually act like that with men."

He ran his fingers through her hair, smoothing it against her neck. Then his hand caressed her slender throat. "And I don't usually come on with the caveman tactics."

Under her half-closed lids, Amber glanced up at him, her pulse leaping when she saw his gaze lingering upon her mouth. "We seem to bring out the worst in each other," she murmured.

His fingertips moved sensuously against her skin. Then he tilted her face toward his. "It's awfully powerful, whatever it is."

"Definitely more than I can handle," she whispered.

"You need to have more faith in yourself," he chided, bringing her close to him. His breath was like a warm caress.

"How can I? One minute we're fighting. The next we're..."

"We're loving," he finished for her.

His voice was honey. His touch, fire. Her own response was wildness.

He folded her completely into his arms. His lips covered hers. Once again she knew the heady exhilaration of his hard mouth devouring her own. Once again she was enveloped in that white-hot searing flame that meant desire. Jake parted her lips and began a sensual exploration of her mouth that drew a low moan of shuddering ecstasy from the depths of her soul. At her tiny sob of surrender, his arms crushed her against his body even more tightly.

"Jake...Jake... What's happening to us?" she cried out.

"The real question is, why are you so determined to keep it from happening?" he replied. At her troubled look, his own expression softened. "Never mind. You don't have to answer."

Then he pressed her bright head against his chest, holding her possessively against him. She could hear the rushing of his heart even as she grew aware of the frenzied rhythm of her own, but she did not pull away. It was too wonderful being in his arms. A magic, sublime peace held them in thrall for a timeless space, an enchanted warm moment of clinging one to the other, a private miracle that belonged to them alone.

When his harsh, uneven breathing grew more natural, Amber slowly pushed herself away from him, though her hands lingered around his waist.

"Amber, from now on, I'm willing to let you set the terms of our relationship."

"Oh, Jake..." She couldn't go on. She was too deeply touched. Just as he was about to embrace her again, a powerful white car came up the drive and braked right behind the horse trailer attached to Jake's truck.

Amber pulled free of Jake's arms and stared miserably at the gleaming Cadillac and the tall brown-haired man stepping out of it. She had completely forgotten about Jim.

Jake turned, too, comprehension dawning. Jim was an old friend, and Jake had recognized his car instantly. "What's Thompson doing here?" he demanded in a hard voice.

"Oh, dear. I'm afraid Jim's come after me."

"What?"

"I have a date with him."

"Tonight?"

She nodded.

"So you put that nightgown on for him?"

"It's not a nightgown."

"It damn sure looks like one."

"With your dirty mind, I'm not surprised you think so."

"Oh, so we're back to that, are we, Miss Purity in the see-through dress, the girl with a fancy for watching naked men through her binoculars? Well, you two have fun. Not that you need my blessing." Jake's blazing eyes ran the length of her body in a fierce, stripping gaze. "It's obvious you intended to the minute you started getting ready for your date."

Rage drowned out all her other emotions. She sputtered in fury, "Yes, yes, I did! And I will have fun! And if only I never have to see you again, this will be the happiest day of my life!''

''It's always a pleasure to make someone's day.'' Jake's dark face was grim. ''Even yours.'' His savage smile grew even grimmer. ''I'll leave Golden in the barn before I go.'' He turned on his heel and stalked down the drive without even nodding toward Jim.

She glared at him. Jake was arrogant! Insufferable! Dictatorial! The very last kind of man she should have anything to do with.

Amber watched him go, and never had she felt more pain than she did as Jake Kassidy walked out of her life for good.

Chapter Seven

Oh, it made perfect sense to Amber that she was better off if she never saw Jake Kassidy again! Just as it made perfect sense that she allow herself to grow as a person, and take care of her financial problems, before she became involved with another man.

Why was it that this ever-so-logical decision about Jake was so difficult to live with? Why did she feel this awful sense of loss?

Why was it that, having decided to avoid him altogether, Amber seemed to run into him everywhere?

Even on the day she and Serena had driven to Vail, and Sheila had stunned Amber by agreeing to market Amber's jewelry in her exclusive shop, Jake had just happened to be in Vail too. He just happened to be coming out of a realtor's office near the clock tower, a briefcase tucked under his arm, when Amber, flushed with pride, flung open the glass door of Sheila's shop.

Amber scarcely noticed Vail's quaint mock-Tyrolean charm. Nor was she aware of the tourists jostling her as she headed toward the café where she was to meet Serena, who had left Amber to discuss the final business details. Amber was floating on a wave of euphoria, remembering Sheila's lavish praise. Certain sentences and phrases stood out.

"Unique talent. You're so original, dear girl. I'm overwhelmed. I want everything you do, dear girl. Everything."

Amber was the one who was overwhelmed.

A fat man in flowered shorts and a red see-through visor bumped into her, and she would have fallen against a planter filled with velvet-bright pansies if someone had not grabbed her elbow.

From behind her the all-too-familiar resonance of a male voice shattered her blissful mood.

"You look happy, Amber. Been spending money or making it?"

Amber whirled, and there stood Jake in a brown corduroy jacket that emphasized the broadness of his shoulders, and a green turtleneck that made his eyes seem even more vividly green than usual.

Her stomach twisted into knots, but she fought to appear calm. She felt vulnerable, and not nearly as indifferent as she longed to be. Her smile had faded the instant she realized the bronzed hand on her arm was his.

"Making it!" she said defensively. "Or at least trying to. Not that it's any of your business!" Oh, why couldn't she at least pretend to be nonchalant?

He steered her beneath the gable of a cottage out of the stream of tourists before removing his hand. "Hey, don't act so glad to see me," he said smoothly, though a bitter grimace chased across his mouth.

She backed against the wall and he leaned toward her, his body separated from hers by mere inches. His eyes burned, and seemed to brand her everywhere they touched. Her gaze devoured him with equal intensity.

"All right, I won't." Her frown deepened. She felt awkward and shy, and achingly aware of him as a man. She caught the scent of him. She yearned for him, for his touch, for his tenderness. And she hated him because she couldn't hate him.

"So Sheila likes your jewelry? I'm glad, Amber. I know how much that means to you."

She felt inordinately pleased that he seemed happy for her. That he shared the pleasure of her success made it all the more meaningful.

"I wish I could say things were going as well for me," he said with a frown, "but I've been having a hell of a time lately with a resort I'm trying to develop. One of my partners may not be able to come up with his share of the money."

"Oh, Jake, I'm sorry." It upset her to think of him having financial worries. She felt herself softening toward him. Then she realized the danger of such misplaced feelings. She should not be sharing anything with him. Nor should she let herself feel concern for him.

Her expression froze. What could she say? What should she do? "I thought we weren't going to have any more to do with one another."

"That was your idea, not mine, remember?" he replied softly. "And I'm afraid it's not working for me. What I wonder is, is it working any better for you?"

He sounded calm and controlled, and she fought to pretend she felt calm too. Yet there was an indefinable current crackling in the air between them.

"At the time, you didn't offer any objections," she managed.

"No." He smiled. "I was too mad at you."

A sudden gust of wind whirled around them. He reached up and gently brushed a fly-away tendril of hair from her eyes. There was something loving and intensely passionate in the gesture. Something that made her ache for so much more than this casual touch, even as he drew his hand away.

He was staring deep into her eyes, and she was sure he saw her hunger for him.

"You had no right to get so angry just because I had a date with another man," she whispered.

"Maybe not. But then, you have a terrible talent for arousing me. And I don't mean just sexual passion, but other passions as well."

His voice was so beautiful, or was it just beautiful to her because it was his?

"Jake, no..."

"I keep assuming all sorts of rights where you're concerned, when I know I shouldn't. You seem to affect me deeply whether I want you to or not."

She blushed. "You want me. You don't want any other man to want me. Yet you don't really want to want me."

He smiled. A sweet, touching smile that was hauntingly beautiful on his face. "You're right about one thing. There are an awful lot of 'wants' between us. Our relationship is a bit of a paradox."

"Wrong, Jake. You and I don't have a relationship."

"Are you so sure about that, Amber? Or do you keep thinking of me, the way I keep thinking of you?"

Jade-green eyes were studying her, but she avoided meeting them.

She hesitated for an instant before giving him her answer. His voice was like velvet, and the passion in his eyes wove a magic spell. His nearness made her want to arch her body into his, to know again blistering contact with those corded, masculine muscles. She wanted to melt into him, to know the comfort of him as well as the passion.

Her fingertips reached hesitantly toward his mouth, so desperately did she long to touch him, to know the pleasure, however brief, of his lips against her flesh.

Then she thought of Don, and she withdrew those traitorous fingers and curled them into a painful fist behind her back.

She wouldn't be free until she had taken care of her obligations to Don, and it would hardly be fair to involve Jake in the mess she'd made of her life. Besides, she was too unsure of herself, and of her needs and motives, to let herself date Jake.

"I'm sure, Jake," she said at last. "I really don't think it's wise for us to have anything more to do with each other."

For a long moment he gravely studied her tortured face, wanting to understand her reasons for denying him.

"Are you so against me because I wanted a relationship without commitments? Is that one mistake going to cost me you?"

"No, Jake. I know you were hurt by someone else and you're not ready to care again. I don't blame you for the way you feel."

"Then why?"

"Maybe part of it is that I can't handle any more relationships without commitments. Maybe I've finally learned that when two people can't care enough to make real investments in each other, they don't have anything together worth having. You were hurt because you loved. I was hurt because I didn't. I don't want to use you, Jake, and I don't want to be used either. And besides all that, there are reasons that have nothing to do with us, but I just can't tell you about them. Not yet, anyway. Is that so impossible to accept?"

"Do I really have a choice?"

She drew a deep shuddering breath. "No."

"If you change your mind, Amber, you know where to find me," he said at last in a quiet voice.

"I won't be changing it."

"What can I say, then? Only that I hope you're wrong. If you ever need me, Amber, even as a friend, I want to help you. You're very special to me."

Then he leaned forward, and she felt his mouth brush her forehead. The kiss was meant to be light and gentle, a sweet farewell between two people who could have been lovers but would never be. But as he drew away from her, Amber pulled him back hungrily. She buried her face in his broad chest and clung to him tightly, finding a sublime contentment and comfort in the hard warmth of him. His arms closed around her, and she felt his terrible wanting.

He let her hold him until she was ready to let him go. Her heart was drumming painfully in her ears as she pulled away. Her soul was in her eyes.

He clenched her fingers in his, the only part of their bodies that still touched. "Amber?" he begged hoarsely.

"Go quickly, Jake." One tear spilled down her cheek.

More than anything, what she wanted was for him to kiss her. To feel his mouth on hers, his arms around her again, the press of his tough, muscled body against hers.

For an instant his grip tightened to iron intensity.

"Please, Jake," she whispered, pressing his palm against her mouth, her lips lingering on callused fingers. "Go before I tell you to stay."

There was an agony in him as profound as her own.

It made him furious that she was rejecting him. "I hope you know what you're doing, woman," he ground out savagely.

When she didn't answer, he tore his eyes from hers. Then, brutally, he wrenched his hands free and broke their embrace. He bolted away from her and vanished quickly in the crowd. For a long time she remained slumped against the wall, lost in her private inlet of despair as the steady stream of tourists flowed past her.

Afterward, Amber relived that scene many times. She couldn't forget the agony in Jake's hard, insolent face just before he'd thrust himself away from her. It had been difficult for him to leave her, but no more difficult than it had been for her to give him up. He couldn't understand, and he despised her because he couldn't.

She began to go out regularly with Jim in an attempt to forget Jake, but it didn't help. Several times when she was with Jim, she ran into Jake, and he was always with a different beautiful woman. Had she been fooling herself to believe she had meant so much to him?

These encounters were always painful for Amber. She would smile awkwardly, or say hello when she was forced to. Sometimes Jake would introduce her to the woman he was with, as if he deliberately wanted to prove he had no further need of Amber. Sometimes he would nod curtly, and then leave quickly with his arm wrapped possessively around his date. Whatever happened, it was almost impossible for Amber to put on a brave face and pretend she didn't care.

Amber spent long, arduous hours in her shop. The more creations she produced, the more Sheila demanded.

"Do something with snowflakes, dear girl."

And after that: "Colorado wildflowers would be lovely, dear girl."

They sold just as quickly as everything else.

Amber's bank account began to build, and she was able to fantasize about sending Don a large check in the future. While Amber worked at creating jewelry and saving money, Serena thought of ingenious ways to promote her. One day, she had Amber sit at a little table in front of Sheila's store signing autographs and passing out little booklets that explained her jewelry-making techniques.

Serena and Amber fought constantly over Serena's ideas for publicity. Serena wanted to have articles written about Amber in the local papers, but Amber was afraid that the wrong people might read them and find out where she was.

One night Jim took Amber to a friend's party in Breckenridge. The setting was a fabulous ski chalet that clung to a mountainside, commanding a magnificent view of the valley. When Jim left her alone to get her a drink, Amber wandered outside onto a balcony and looked at the mountains. She hadn't felt like making small talk with strangers.

Beneath her she could see the gleam of the Blue River, and on its banks the shadowy ridges of washed stones and gravel. These were the waste-heaps of gold dredges that had worked in the area as recently as 1942.

It was late summer, and the night air was crisp and cool, smelling of aromatic pine and spruce. There was a quietness, a serenity to the evening.

Through the half-opened door she could hear the murmur of the party going on without her, the beat of the band. Outside there was the quiet, and the silver moonlight dusting the uppermost boughs of the trees and slanting across the meadows.

Never had she felt more alone. It had been two months since she'd given Jake up, and she still yearned for him as terribly as ever.

A black shadow fell across the balcony. From behind her there was a sound. Then a man whose voice she recognized instantly called to her.

"Amber..."

At first she thought the husky whisper was a dream. She turned and saw the dark figure of a man silhouetted against the brilliance of the party, an ebony candle in the middle of its afterglow. Jake pushed the glass door open a little wider and stepped outside.

He was elegant and dashing in a black suit and tie.

Suddenly the blood was pounding behind her ears.

"Why, Jake, what are you doing out here?" she managed, a little breathlessly.

"Looking for you."

He handed her a drink. The tips of their fingers touched, and she jumped back a little too quickly, her green chiffon gown swirling around her. The dress clung to her, outlining the shape of her body.

He stood there, looking at her, drinking in the sight of her. Though he said nothing, something in his eyes told her he found her very beautiful.

Amber lifted her glass and sipped. Scotch burned all the way down her throat. She quickly set her glass down on a little table against the wall.

He drained his drink in a single draft.

"H—how did you know I was here?"

He set his glass beside hers.

"I saw Jim inside, alone. I asked a friend to monopolize him a bit."

"A beautiful woman, I imagine."

He smiled. "My date."

"You've been having a lot of those lately."

"Look who's talking."

"You shouldn't leave her alone too long."

"I don't intend to."

He grinned down at her, that devastating grin she'd never been able to resist. And all she could do was stare mutely into his eyes, unable to tear her gaze from the masculine splendor of his face.

Had God designed him expressly to appeal to her? The nighttime darkness accentuated the blackness of his hair and the whiteness of his teeth.

For an instant his hands drew her attention. She noticed how white the cuffs of his shirt were against his large olive hands. She studied the wisps of curling black hair on them. They were the hands of a large male animal. They were powerful, and yet they knew how to be beguilingly gentle. She remembered their touch, and the memory alone stirred her far too much.

Fleetingly her eyes rose to his again, and she thought he could read her every thought.

Never had he seemed more virile, nor more vitally exciting. Nor more dangerous.

"How's the resort going?" she asked, seeking an impersonal topic.

"Not too good."

He ended that subject without ever letting it begin.

"I'm sorry to hear that, Jake." Her gaze trailed miserably to his lips and then away. She clenched the railing behind her for support.

"You're putting us both through hell," came the soft voice. "You know that, don't you, Amber?"

She bit into her top lip and stared, first at him and then down at her toes, trying to concentrate on the way the rhinestones on her shoes sparkled like bits of stardust, but really thinking only of him.

"Why does it make sense for you to date Jim when you won't date me?"

"He's only a friend," she mumbled.

She felt the caress of his fingertip beneath her chin, and she shivered at the tingling rush of excitement that swept through her. He tilted her face back and studied her.

"Isn't that just another way of saying he's someone you aren't willing to make a commitment to?"

His deep voice was the most dangerous of all melodies. His eyes mesmerized her as they moved over her body, burning her skin just as if he had touched her with his hand. His palm trailed down her smooth, white throat, and every nerve ending quivered in response.

"Jake, don't."

"Aren't you using him?" Jake's hand moved lower, caressing her bare shoulder. She shuddered. "You're still running away from what's real, aren't you, Amber?"

"No."

"Then tell me why you chose him over me."

Jake's work-roughened fingers played with the tips of her silken hair. Then he smoothed it back from her face and circled her throat with his fingers. Beneath his thumb he felt the rapid murmur of her pulse.

"It's more complicated than that, and you know it!"

She whirled away and would have run inside, but he grabbed her by the arm and pulled her back hard against him, holding her so tightly their bodies seemed to merge into one. She felt the burning heat of his thigh against her own.

"I want an answer, damn it. Why couldn't you choose me?"

"I don't know."

"Do you have any idea what it does to me to see you out with him? To imagine the two of you alone? To imagine him kissing you? When I want all those things so badly?"

"Jake."

"I can't stand it anymore," he whispered, his voice thick with passion. For a long moment he buried his face in her hair, savoring the rich, perfumed softness of it. "You're driving me crazy."

She reached tentatively toward him and traced her finger along the sandpaper roughness of his cheek before she remembered she shouldn't touch him.

She pulled her hand away. She was afraid. Of him. Of herself. Of all her old needs and wants. Of the new ones that might bring a new kind of failure and pain. All her life she had wanted the security of a loving relationship. Once Don had seemed to offer her that emotional security. Now Jim made her feel safe because with him she didn't feel vulnerable. But Jake... He was both agony and ecstasy, and she no longer knew if he represented danger or deliverance.

For now there was only the darkness of the night. Only the flame in Jake's eyes. Only the velvet heat of his hands moving over her body, and the answering excitement inside herself.

More than anything she wanted to run, but somehow she couldn't as he crushed her tightly into his arms. Her senses were assaulted by the musky, masculine scent of him, by the all-enveloping warmth of his body, by the power of him as man that welcomed her as woman.

He wound his hands in the thick masses of her hair and pulled her face up to his, capturing her lips. There were no more words between them. No more will left in her to resist him.

He tasted faintly, pleasantly, of whiskey. As his lips pressed hungrily down onto hers, opening them to his demanding tongue, Amber melted into him, dizzy and breathless from the force of his passion, shyly, tentatively letting her tongue mate with his.

A tremor shook him at her response, and he wrapped her in his arms even more tightly than before, as if to make her one with his flesh. There was the fusion of skin against skin, of mouth on mouth, of body into body. For a long, rapturous moment they were aware of nothing except their intense, compelling need for each other.

Amber was falling into a wild black whirlpool of passion. There seemed nothing left of herself, no part of her that did not belong to him.

There was only Jake and the strength of his arms holding her against his shaking body, the torrid heat of his mouth devouring hers, the fire of his emotion sweeping her away in a whirl of flood tide and fire.

She was surrendering to a force more powerful than any she'd ever known before. It was like dying, this totality of giving and needing.

Never before had she felt such loss of self, and she was afraid. Afraid to lose herself to a power she couldn't control, that might take her places she shouldn't go. So, only half-knowing what she did, she pushed him away. Panic made her beat against his chest with her hands. Wildly she tore herself free of him, pushing him so hard he stumbled back against the glass door.

For a long moment he just stared at her, his breath coming in a series of sharp, agonized rasps, his eyes blazing with desire as he tried to make sense of her rejection.

"I don't want you!" she cried desperately. In that moment she would have done anything, said anything to stop him. "What do I have to do to make you understand that! I hate you for the way you keep chasing after me like some poor lovesick mongrel when I never want to see you again!"

He winced, and the light in his eyes died, her hateful words having cut him to the quick because he was still crazy with desire for her. "Lovesick mongrel." The phrase tormented him.

Hurt was a blade from hell ripping his gut wide open, but he made no cry of pain. The wound went too deep.

He swallowed against the bitter bile that clogged his throat.

His eyes darkened in his ashen face.

For a long tense moment there was silence. Then his voice sliced through the darkness, low and strangled.

"You're wrong. I don't want you. And I'll never bother you again."

She turned wretchedly away from him, but she was aware of his retreating footsteps, aware of his voice inside the chalet as he politely claimed his date and said his goodbyes.

All the strength seemed to go out of her. She kept remembering how proud and haggard he'd looked as he'd tried to conceal his pain.

Then a door slammed, and she knew he was gone.

There was only the low throb of the music, the vast star-spangled emptiness of the night, and an utter aloneness within herself.

Chapter Eight

During the next four weeks, Sheila kept demanding more new creations, and Amber had to drive herself relentlessly to produce them. Summer gave way to fall, and the days shortened and grew colder.

In the mountains, September snow dusted the granite peaks, and the aspens turned to gold. David came home from camp and started back to school, and Serena seemed more settled after his return.

After the party in Breckenridge, Amber stopped dating Jim. She didn't want to use him as Jake had accused her of doing. Nor did she want to risk another encounter with Jake.

All she knew of Jake, beyond the emptiness in her heart, was what Hamlin or Serena told her.

One morning over coffee, Serena said, "It's a good thing you didn't come with us to the party last night, Amber darling. Jake was there, and he had another beautiful brunette on his arm. Didn't I tell you he collects women like some men collect hunting trophies? You remember last week we told you that we saw him with that cute little blonde.''

Amber's throat seemed to close, and it was hard to breathe, much less speak. At last she managed a faint rasping sound that didn't sound like her voice at all.

"Serena, I don't care who Jake dates…er…collects.''

Serena shot her a look that made Amber feel she was about as difficult to see through as cellophane.

It was a lie, of course, when Amber said she didn't care about Jake.

Would she never forget the exact color of those vivid green eyes? Never get over the sick longing to have his hard arms clamp around her again and press her tightly to him? How many nights had she lain in her bed, half-asleep, half-awake, dreaming of him, longing to feel his body tremble with passion she had aroused?

"Then you probably aren't interested in the fact that Jake is having quite a few problems with that new resort he's building outside of Steamboat Springs. I understand one of his partners backed out, and Jake has to come up with a great deal more money than he expected. Money I hear he doesn't have.''

In spite of everything, Amber hated the thought of Jake being in trouble. Aloud she said, "Please, Serena, I really don't want to hear about Jake. Not about his women or his problems.''

"Sorry, I thought you'd be interested,'' Serena murmured.

Beneath Serena's thoughtful gaze, Amber grew uncomfortable. She got up and went to the sink, but when she stared out the window toward the mountains, the sight only intensified the memories of Jake. The Kassidy Ranch lay in that direction, and Jake was probably out there somewhere on Frisco.

She set her cup and saucer down. Then she fled the kitchen, and Serena, to seek the solitude of her shop.

All day Amber worked feverishly. She felt lost and homesick, and she almost wished she could once again be the fairy-tale girl on her wind-kissed island in the Caribbean, the simple girl who had thought she was happy with material success and her shallow marriage.

She used the shape of shells for inspiration that afternoon and twisted gold into abstract designs. When she was finished, she had created a wonderful necklace with a bold modern pendant. Had her mother been alive, Amber would have presented it to her in the hope of winning her approval. Amber decided to give it to Serena as a gift.

It was nearly six when Amber returned to the house. Thinking she might ride Golden later, she went to her room and put on her oldest jeans and a navy sweatshirt. Then she pinned her hair up into a knot on the top of her head.

Amber went down to the kitchen, where Paula was bustling about preparing Hamlin's favorite meal—fried chicken, homemade currant jelly, creamed onions and garden lettuce. The warm scent of baking bread made Amber's stomach growl as she poured herself a cup of hot tea.

She snitched a piece of lettuce from the salad, dipped it in Italian dressing and munched until Paula began to scold. Then, grabbing one last piece of lettuce on the run, Amber took her tea and a folded newspaper outside.

She threw herself down on the porch swing beside a trellis laden with the last of the sweet peas. She often sat on the porch in the evening to enjoy the dazzling display of light and shadow as it worked its wondrous magic on the clouds, the desert and the mountains.

Intending to relax, she lay back, opened the newspaper and gave a startled little yelp.

On the front page was an immense black-and-white photograph of herself. The sun was on her face, the wind in her hair. She'd been riding Golden when Serena had snapped the shot.

Electrified, Amber bolted into a sitting position, her own smile as frozen as the one in the picture.

"No..." she whispered. "No."

Beneath the photograph, the headline read, "Local artisan achieves astonishing success with her jewelry-making."

She bit into her bottom lip and moaned aloud, "Serena, how could you?"

Amber read the article, her trembling hands gripping the newspaper. She was terrified. The article might be reprinted in some other newspaper. There was no predicting who might see it. No predicting what the men to whom she and Don owed money might do to her.

Slowly Amber refolded the newspaper. She sat there, studying the serrated mountain peaks long after the last ray of fire had died, long after night cloaked them with sparkling velvet blackness.

Later, Amber showed Serena the newspaper.

Serena was proudly expectant. "Of course I've seen it, Amber darling."

"I asked you not to."

"But I knew you were just being shy. I thought you'd be thrilled."

"Well, I'm not. You mustn't ever, ever do anything like this again."

"But you're being ridiculous, darling."

"Serena, I realize you're only trying to help, but believe me, this will only hurt me."

"I don't see how."

And Amber couldn't bring herself to explain.

She jammed her hands into her pockets and rocked back on her heels, silently praying she was wrong.

"Just this once listen to me, Serena."

"All right."

"Promise me you'll never do anything like this again."

Serena hesitated. She looked hurt and vulnerable, and Amber felt a pang of guilt.

"It's very important to me, Serena. If you don't, I'll have to go away. And I don't even know where I'd go."

At last Serena managed an imperceptible nod.

The article was reprinted in the Denver papers, and shortly after that the nightmare began.

At first there were only a few telephone calls. If Amber answered, a man made threats and demanded money. If anyone else answered, the line went dead.

Hamlin had the telephone number changed, and the calls stopped. For a while. Then they began all over again.

Strangely, in time, Amber grew used to them. When nothing else happened, Amber's fears began to recede, a false sense of security lulling her nerves.

One cold sun-bright morning Amber borrowed Serena's Corvette and drove to Vail to pick up a check from Sheila and to give her more designs. It was one of those perfect crystal days Colorado is so famous for, the kind of day that inspires a sense of miraculous well-being in every living creature.

White trails of jets crisscrossed a cobalt-blue sky. The mountains were shimmering gold every time the wind stirred the quaking aspens.

Amber parked the Corvette in a parking garage and got out, paying no attention to the black Lincoln that pulled into the garage just as she was leaving. She walked briskly through the nearly empty streets toward Sheila's exclusive shop, unaware of the pale blond man behind her. Unaware of the pale intent eyes watching her.

The summer tourists were gone, but there was still a sprinkling of bearded youths and lank-haired lasses lounging in immaculate Vail doorways, absorbing its ambience of freedom.

Amber stopped to buy a bag of rich, dark chocolate candy for Paula from her favorite chocolate shop. Then she window-shopped. She went into a shop and tried on a sheepskin jacket and matching hat that looked so wonderful on her she was tempted to part with some of her savings—until she remembered she wanted to give everything to Don.

It felt so good to be out in the fresh air after being cooped up in her shop for so many days. There was no hint of danger. Nothing in the beautiful day to set her on edge. Nothing to warn her.

Until, as Sheila was making out her check, Amber looked up and noticed a plain potato of a man in a black raincoat peering over the pots of red geraniums through the window.

Then she knew!

He was short and stocky, plumpish, and yet there was no softness to him. Tinted wire-rimmed glasses glinted in the sunlight, concealing his eyes. He was losing his pale blond hair. He had the sort of skin that burns and never tans, and he was slightly sunburned, as if he'd just recently come from some far-flung southern isle.

He was not looking at the jewelry. Through the dark glasses he was studying her. There was something chillingly familiar about him. She had met him once somewhere with Don, and though he was the kind of man she wouldn't have expected to remember, she had.

The plump pale-faced man smiled wetly, and fear seeped through her. Her legs buckled, and she grasped the glass counter for support. Two items of jewelry fell soundlessly to the carpet and lay upon red plush, glittering and forgotten.

Sheila looked up and saw that Amber's face was bloodless.

"Are you all right?"

"I—I'm fine. That man at the window. I thought for a minute I knew him."

Sheila squinted, then lowered her bifocals so she could see over them.

The street outside was empty. "Well, he seems to be gone now."

"Y—yes."

But he wasn't.

He was standing on the corner eating an ice-cream cone in the bright sunshine when Amber came out of Sheila's shop. The minute Amber saw him she began to run. Blindly, panicked, she scrambled past tourists, past the lavish shops.

He dashed his cone on the pavement and ran after her. The melting strawberry ice cream oozed into the cracks of the sidewalk like congealed blood.

Amber stumbled through the streets. She could hear the thunder of his footsteps closing on her. There was a series of loud crashes. Heavy furniture toppled and fell.

Vases shattered on cement, their flowers spilling, and she realized he'd knocked over several tables and chairs in front of a sidewalk café.

There were angry shouts.

"Hey, mister. Why don't you watch where you're going!"

Amber was panting breathlessly. Sharp pains knifed through her lungs.

He was right behind her, relentlessly pursuing her.

He caught her near the ski lift and slammed her against a low wall. When she tried to scream, he covered her mouth with his hand.

Insane terror rose in her throat like a choking hot fluid.

Somewhere there was the sound of children's laughter. A red ball bounced on a distant green lawn, and a boy and girl went chasing after it.

Those sounds belonged to another world.

Amber was hypnotized with fear. The man's thin mouth twisted into a damp grimace. His terrible eyes held triumph. One of his hands was on her throat. "You're coming with me, and if you don't do what I say, I'll hurt you."

Amber was too terrified to listen, too desperate to escape him. Frantically she tried to pull away, kicking again, twisting her body. She grabbed his glasses and ripped them from his face.

His expert hands clamped down hard on her elbow, grinding bone into muscle and nerve in exactly the right place to produce pain that was so sudden and excruciating she almost fainted. A shaft of fire went up her arm and paralyzed her neck and shoulder. She stopped struggling, and allowed him to pull her forward toward the concrete stairwell that led down to the parking garage.

"If you don't walk down these steps with me," he whispered in a chilling monotone, "and act like nothing's wrong, I won't just fool around the next time. I'll really break your arm. I'll do more than that, if you push me."

Her arm felt as limp and numb as if he'd already broken it. She looked into those cold colorless eyes. He would hurt her. He might even kill her, and he wouldn't mind doing it.

"You're going to get in my car, and we're going to drive somewhere where we can talk," he commanded.

"I'll talk here," she pleaded with him, terrified of what he might do to her if he got her alone.

"No."

He dragged her down the stairs into the darkened garage. One hand was a vise-like claw gripping her wrist while he unlocked the door of his Lincoln. Just as he was about to shove her inside, a police car happened into the garage.

For a moment they both stared at it stupefied. Then Amber screamed, and the scream echoed and reverberated off the concrete walls.

Her kidnapper loosened his grip, and she managed to yank free, slam her foot down hard on his instep, and run toward her own car.

Instead of chasing after her, her abductor raced up the stairs and escaped.

One of the officers got out of the patrol car and strode officiously over to Amber as she was letting herself into her car. He was tall, redheaded and stout, and very glad of something to do.

"You all right, little lady?"

She turned wildly. Her hair was half down, half up. Her face was flushed, her eyes brilliant. There were red marks all over one arm. Her sleeve was torn.

"I—I'm great," she replied breathlessly.

He tilted his cap back from his brow, and his forehead seemed to sprout carrot curls. He raised a skeptical red eyebrow. "Yeah, and I'm the Jolly Green Giant."

She didn't want to involve the police.

"R-really, I'm fine. I—I thought I saw a rat over by those water pipes, that's all."

"A human rat, I'll bet."

She stared at him silently. She wasn't about to confirm his suspicions.

The officer smiled. "I'd hate to hear you scream if someone was really trying to hurt you. Though I can't imagine how it could be much louder."

Amber clenched the door handle. He didn't know how right he was. There was a sick feeling in the pit of her stomach—the remnants of her subsiding terror.

The light had gone out of the crystal day as Amber turned off the four-lane highway onto the narrow black ribbon of asphalt that wound over mountains and desert to Hamlin's ranch.

Menacing purple-black clouds skirted blood-red slopes. Sinister shadows darkened the barren hillsides.

For the first time, Amber noticed a black Lincoln in her rearview mirror. It signaled, and made the same turn she had.

No! It couldn't be!

But it was.

Her foot pressed down on the accelerator, and the Corvette shot forward with a burst of speed.

The Lincoln loomed inexorably in her mirror.

It began to rain, great pelting raindrops spattering onto her windshield.

Amber switched on the wipers and drove faster. Faster than she'd ever driven. And more dangerously.

Tires screamed around curves, then hissed on wet asphalt when the road straightened. Gravel plunged down mountain slopes when she skidded.

The sports-car climbed effortlessly, the Lincoln with more difficulty.

She was losing him. Gradually. But when she came out of the mountains, into the desert . . .

The rain was a drumming tattoo of heart-stopping fear.

The pungent odor of damp sage invaded the Corvette. With every mile the vistas grew broader, the land drier.

High above her in the mountains there was no rain. A dusty ruffle of road climbed the jagged slopes. A hawk made lazy circles against heavenly blue.

The Corvette swept over the top of the pass; the Lincoln was no longer visible.

But it was there. Behind her. Unseen, and monstrous.

The mountain road was a zigzag. A terrifying roller coaster as it swooped and coiled over granite precipices.

Amber came out of the mountains. As abruptly as the rain had started, it stopped.

The Lincoln was behind her, a black speck in the distance.

She sped through a village beside the river. A little nothing of a town.

Trailers were nestled beneath willows. The valley was large, irrigated. Dry creek beds, choked with brush, fanned out from the river.

Children and their dog gawked from the doorstep of a squat red tar-paper cabin beside the highway as Amber roared past them.

The speck was growing larger in her rearview mirror, like an inkblot seeping into paper toweling.

There was no escape.

No matter how fast she drove, he would catch her.

She missed the road to Hamlin's ranch, and took the one right after it.

She flew past a large white sign with bold black-and-gilt lettering that read, "Kassidy Ranch.

She flew past a white horse, and a man who was kneeling beside a calf.

As Jake rose slowly, the black Lincoln swerved past him.

Amber gasped. The Lincoln was immense in her rearview mirror. She pushed down on the accelerator, but it was no use.

Metal scraped against metal as the Lincoln crashed into her rear bumper. Shoving. Crumpling.

The Corvette bolted forward and skidded. Amber gripped the steering wheel, struggling for control as the Lincoln rammed into her again.

Ahead the road became gravel. And it curved.

She would never make it if she didn't slow down.

But she couldn't slow down.

He hit her again, harder than before. And then again, from a different angle. Tires tried to grab, but there was no asphalt to grab. Only flying rocks.

He was going to kill her!

The Corvette spun out of control.

The car whirled and tipped crazily in slow motion.

Amber's hoarse, keening scream rent the air.

It was a moment of madness. The wildest carnival ride of Amber's life, only a thousand times more terrifying.

Then she slammed head-on into a boulder.

Despite her shoulder harness, her head crashed into the steering wheel.

And no matter how hard she fought not to, she felt herself sliding into nothingness.

Amber regained consciousness as the blond man was dragging her out of the Corvette. Her first awareness was of a white-hot burning on her temple, of an intolerable agony in her right shoulder every time her jerked her.

Her eyes fluttered open, but it was difficult to focus. Her hearing was just as fuzzy. The man's labored grunts as he struggled to pull her body across leather upholstery were faint and indistinct.

She was only vaguely aware of the danger of the man as he leaned over her, but when he tried to hoist her over his shoulder and carry her toward the Lincoln, the sudden impact of her injured shoulder against his arm made her scream with pain.

She clawed wildly and kicked at him. Tufts of blond hair came away in her fingers.

''Bitch!''

He hurled her down onto the ground. She hit the rocky earth so hard it knocked her breathless, and she was too stunned to try to move away as he dropped on top of her.

He pulled her against his body, and pain coursed through her in waves. She closed her eyes in terror and despair.

"Let me go," she whispered. "Please."

"Not till I get what I came for."

"What do you want?"

"Money."

"I don't have any."

"Then you'll get it, or I'll take you back to the Bahamas to my boss. Since you left, Lynn hasn't paid us a cent. Maybe if I take you back, we can use you for an incentive."

"I—I'll pay you what I can, but I won't let you use me to blackmail Don."

"The hell you won't." He balled his hand into a fist.

She squeezed her eyes shut, seeming to cower, but her fingers slid over the dirt and found a large, smooth rock. She raised it, but she didn't have to hit him, because his fist never crashed downward toward her delicate cheekbone.

A brown hand had wrapped around the man's wrist like a manacle and held it poised in midair.

"Just what do you think you're doing, mister?" Jake asked softly, twisting the clenched hand back viciously.

"It's none of your business," the pale man hissed.

"Yeah? Well, this is my ranch, and that makes it my business."

Suddenly they were fighting. Jake threw the pale man to the ground, where they wrestled and rolled over and over in the dirt. Jake attacked him like a demon, his fists pounding into the other man's mouth.

The pale blonde's lip split, and blood spurted out.

"You dirty bastard," the stranger snarled, wiping the blood away with the back of his hand. His colorless eyes narrowed. He reached into his belt and drew a gun. Then he brought it down hard against Jake's cheek, and Jake staggered to the ground.

The stranger raised the gun to hit Jake again.

Amber's hand closed around the rock and she dragged herself toward the two men. She grabbed the stranger's arm, and when he tried to aim the gun at her she hit his hand with the rock, and the automatic fell to the ground.

They both lunged for it, but Jake grabbed the man's legs and held him back. Amber picked up the gun and aimed the shiny black barrel at the man's stomach.

She'd never pointed a gun at a man before, and instead of filling her with a sense of power, it heightened her terror. Her hands shook, and the gun wobbled dangerously. But that only made it more threatening.

"It'll go off if you don't watch what you're doing," the man warned.

"And we wouldn't want that," she whispered. "Get in your car."

Eyeing her warily, the man rose slowly to his feet.

She waved the gun toward the Lincoln. "Now go."

Jake was pulling himself to his feet. The engine roared.

"Amber, you can't just let him get away," Jake yelled, heaving himself toward the tail of the car.

The Lincoln leapt forward and headed down the gravel road, leaving a choking cloud of dust trailing behind it. Only when she was sure the man had gone did she lower the gun. Her numb fingers loosened, and it fell to the ground.

The gun bounced, and there was an explosion. Amber screamed as a bullet zinged past her leg, barely missing Jake, then ricochetted off a rock.

"What the hell?" Jake stormed. "First he hits me with that thing and now you damn near shoot me. Don't you know anything about guns, girl?"

She leaned down to pick up the gun, but Jake's harsh voice stopped her.

"Don't you dare!"

She hesitated and turned toward Jake.

Their eyes met. His held anger, relief and questions. Questions she wasn't ready to answer. She wondered if he could see her fear, if he could read her guilt.

Her chest contracted painfully at the sight of him, and she could feel the tears coming into her eyes. He was rubbing his bruised cheek, but he was all right.

His white shirt hung in tatters, revealing his hard, muscled chest and back. A tumble of dusty black hair fell across his brow. He was so handsome, more than handsome, even though he was covered with red dust and blood seeped from a scratch on his forehead. He was tall and so unutterably virile. Strong and powerful and dashing, yet somehow vulnerable with his bruised face.

He was dearer than she ever could have admitted before.

He'd risked his life to save her, and he'd nearly been killed. She realized how dangerously close she'd come to losing him.

"Jake!" She went to him and flung herself into his arms.

"Amber." His voice was deep and wonderful, though she was aware that he was restraining his emotions just as he was restraining his questions. His hands stroked her hair. "You're one hell of a gunslinger." His fingers were velvet-soft, as they always were when he touched her in a man-woman way. "Who was that man? What did he want?"

"H-he was just someone who followed me home," Amber managed, evading the truth because she didn't want to involve Jake in the mess she'd made of her life.

She felt his fingers knot with tension.

"He was damned determined," Jake said, too smoothly, and she realized he did not believe her.

She could no longer look into his eyes.

"He must have been some sort of maniac," she replied lightly.

"He was a maniac, all right—" came Jake's furious undertone. "I'd give anything to know what the hell he wanted from you. But you're not going to tell me, are you?"

How could she?

"Oh, Jake..." She raised her fingertips to the purple mark. Gently she touched it. She began to sob. Now that the danger was past, she could finally let go.

He held her tightly against him, comforting her, speaking soothingly, curbing his rage. He felt her trembling. She was afraid, and no matter how difficult it was for him not to vent his anger and frustration because she refused to confide in him, she needed his support. Gently he kissed the top of her head. "You're safe now, Amber. Safe." He drew her closer, and slowly his concern for her overpowered his anger.

It was a long time before she could regain control of herself, but at last she wiped the tears from her face and managed to speak. "You were hurt... because of me. I'll never forgive myself for that. When I think of how I treated you, and then you risked your life for me. Thank you, Jake, for what you did."

"Maybe I should be thanking you," he murmured. "You got his gun and kept him from beating my face to a pulp."

"I had no choice."

"Neither did I."

"But I've been so awful to you."

"I never stopped wanting you, Amber." He placed his broad hand on her injured shoulder, and gently traced the delicate curves of her body.

The intimate touch of his hand and the low throb in his voice mesmerized her. "And I never stopped wanting you," she admitted.

The brown hand moved lower, following the shape of her breast. "Don't you think it's time we did something about it?"

"That again," she whispered. "You never give up."

She placed her hand over his, intending to draw it away. Instead he brought her fingers to his lips and kissed each of her fingertips lingeringly, his hot breath blowing between her fingers and sending little shivers through her. "Not when I want something as badly as I want you."

"I'm scared, Jake."

His green eyes were intense. "Does it help to know that I'm just as scared as you?"

"Not much."

"Then maybe this will help."

He pulled her against him, holding her so tightly she could scarcely breathe, and she didn't resist as he lowered his mouth to hers and kissed her. She knew she should have protested, but her body had a will of its own, and her head tipped back to savor the sweet warmth of his mouth. She could feel the bulging muscles of his thighs, the width and depth of his broad shoulders and chest.

He kissed her gently at first. Unconsciously she grasped the cotton tatters of his shirt to pull him closer. Surrender quivered through her limbs, igniting a smoldering heat that melted her bones. Her arms wound around his neck, and she was caught in the fierce enchantment of his male sexuality.

His mouth hardened and became more demanding, and she felt gloriously fulfilled for the first time in months. Her loins went hot and waxen, and she melted into his hard embrace. Her tongue met and matched his, easing tentatively inside his mouth.

Her response drove him wild.

"Amber," he breathed, shuddering.

She was lost in a swirling haze of emotions she had never known existed. She ached for his kisses, for his touch, for his love in an instinctive, primeval way.

All her life she had been searching for love. Until this moment she'd never really believed she could find it.

He rained wild kisses upon her mouth, her throat. His hands dug roughly into the cascades of apricot hair, yet it was a caress. He drank of her, ate of her.

"You belong to me," he murmured.

She could feel the thunder of his heart, the disturbed huskiness of his breathing. She was molded to his body, and the heat in him was a fire that raged inside herself. Her fingertips were coiled tightly in the black thickness of his hair.

She couldn't deny what he said. She didn't even want to.

She bent her head back and pulled his mouth down to hers once more.

"I'm yours," she said. "I have never been anyone else's."

Chapter Nine

Jake was sprawled across his living room couch, and Amber was kneeling beside him, carefully dabbing antiseptic on the cut above his brow.

"Ouch!"

The black head tried to twist out of her reach.

"Quit moving, Jake, or I'll get this stuff in your eyes. Then you'll really have something to cry about."

"That hurts, in case you didn't realize it, Nurse Johnson."

"I never would have known you were such a big sissy, if I hadn't come inside to doctor you."

Her sparkling eyes met his. Then her gaze was drawn to his lips.

Oh, why did the hard, straight line of his mouth beckon her so excitingly?

He grabbed the offending hand and made her stop. At his touch a tremulous wave of longing racked her body. She knew by the sudden blaze in his eyes that he felt it, too.

The wad of cool damp cotton fell from her fingers to the floor.

"There are a lot of things you don't know about me," he murmured.

"But I'm in the mood to learn." Her blue eyes were softly luminous, yet warm.

"You certainly changed your mind in one hell of a hurry." Jake's reply was quietly sardonic.

"It's a woman's prerogative to change her mind, you know."

There was a moment of smoldering silence. Only their eyes seemed to touch. Only their souls.

Then she brought her face down close to his and nuzzled her velvet cheek against the sandpaper roughness of his. The gentle contact was electric. He could feel the tips of her breasts through her thin blouse as they brushed against his chest, and a tremor went through him.

She probably knew exactly what she was doing, he thought.

"I've waited a long time for this moment," he said softly, with a rueful smile.

His hands gently caressed her body as he kissed the tip of her nose lightly.

"What do you mean?"

She leaned over him, slowly lowering her weight on top of him. Her face was taut with passion, her eyes gentle and loving. If her life depended on it, she no longer had the will to resist him.

"Jake—" She breathed his name against his mouth. The blood in her arteries had turned to liquid flame.

Her lips met his, and she was open for him, the way he'd dreamed of her being. With her mouth parted, she let him taste her. Her arms slid around his neck, clutching him, her fingers combing the thick, silken hair at the nape.

Her tongue came out from between her moist lips and explored the firm outline of his mouth.

"You taste delicious," she purred.

Everything she did aroused him. He was trembling against her, his arms shaking as they held her against him, his mouth shaking also as it plundered the gentle sweetness of hers.

Then, suddenly, he stiffened and tore his head away, his breath coming fast and hard.

"Don't you know you're driving me crazy?" he swore softly beneath his breath.

"You're always accusing me of that," she chided seductively. "It doesn't seem to matter what I do."

Jake's mouth formed into that tantalizing smile of his. "Oh, it matters."

Her warm breath fanned the pulse in the hollow of his throat.

Every cell in his body felt hard. "More than you know," he muttered.

On top of him her female body was warm, feather-light, perfumed. Incredibly sexy. Never had he known a woman more alluringly fashioned. He was totally supporting her weight. Not that he minded. Every part of him seemed to be softly enveloped by her yielding womanliness. He wanted to sheath himself inside her, to know her completely, to make her his. He had only to...

His breath caught. He lay as still as a statue. He looked past her, forcing himself to concentrate on the spokes of the western chandelier that looked like a wagon wheel.

"Dear Lord." Surely he was dying.

When he didn't take her mouth again, she kissed his eyelids, his cheeks, his mouth, but he continued to lie motionless under her caresses.

He felt her body embrace his. Her legs lay on top of his. She was firm, long-limbed. He wanted to tear off her clothes, to savor the womanly splendor of her.

The fullness of her breasts pressed against his bare chest. She arched her back and then bent forward, running her tongue from his earlobe, down his throat, to his navel, nibbling and sucking and licking until he caught her to him with a groan, stopping the unbearable eroticism.

"I thought you wanted me to," she whispered, pleading.

She couldn't understand his strange stillness. He was the most beautiful thing in the world to her, his rugged, intensely masculine features and the hard virility of that tough, brown body appealing to her in a way she would never have believed possible.

Her eyes slid shamelessly along those wide, muscled shoulders to where they joined the strong neck, then moved lower over the muscled chest, her gaze burning him as though it were a physical caress.

She let her hair fall upon his chest like a velvet-soft curtain, tickling him, stirring him. She was trembling, eager.

Every sense in his body was feverishly aware of her. He was wild for her, dying for her.

"I do want you to." His voice was thick with unmistakable passion.

"Then?"

"I've wanted you in my debt," he said hoarsely. "Clinging to me. Seeking comfort in my arms. Willing..." His words died away, but the fire in his gaze did not.

"Well, I'm in your debt now. I'll do anything to repay you for saving me."

"Anything?" He drawled the word. "That takes in a lot of territory."

"Oh, I intend to." She let her fingertips trail wantonly over his torso, playing with the dark little ringlets his body hair made in the center of his chest. Her hand moved lower, to the sterling-silver belt buckle with the turquoise inlay. "Tell me exactly what territory you want me to take in."

His body turned to water. Her touch was excruciating, exquisite. It was difficult to think, to speak.

"It's ironic," he began, in a choked voice that didn't sound at all like his own, "but reality has a way of never living up to one's fantasies."

"And what were they?" She laughed throatily.

"Don't ask."

"But Jake—"

"Isn't it enough that I don't want to take advantage of you when you're feeling weak and frightened?"

"I'm not feeling weak and frightened. I'm—"

"Yes, you are, and I refuse to take advantage of you."

"So, Jake, you have a noble streak after all."

"I wouldn't get my hopes up just yet."

"Oh, I wasn't. I'm not in the mood for nobility. I want to make love to you. More than anything."

In all his life, Jake had never turned down a woman he wanted, and he was at a loss to explain himself. He took a deep breath.

Then, very gently, he pushed her away and sat up, turning his back to her. He buried his head in his tautly clenched hands.

For a dazed moment, Amber could only stare at his bent shoulders, at the rumpled blackness of his bent head. She felt abandoned and alone. Aching to be near him, she reached out her hand to console him.

He felt her slight movement on the couch and sensed her intention.

"Don't, Amber." He ground the harsh, trembling words between clenched teeth.

She bit into her lip, almost welcoming the hurt of her teeth cutting soft flesh. She felt engulfed by pain. She'd thrown herself at him, and he wouldn't have her.

"Why?" she whispered, longing desperately to understand. "Did I do something wrong?"

"It's not you, damn it," he growled, raking his hand through his hair. "It's me."

"But . . . you kept saying you wanted me."

"Apparently I don't know what the hell I want anymore."

She stood and tilted her head back. Shaking fingers groped to button her blouse where it had come loose. "Then I'll go." Tears were welling in her eyes.

He saw her stricken look, and he hated himself even more.

She bowed her head in humiliation, not wanting him to see how starved she was for him. Then she ran toward the door.

He sprang from the couch. He caught her just as her fingers closed over the doorknob.

He gripped her hard, arching her body roughly into his as he pushed her against the wall. She cried out, her voice muffled, frightened.

He was shaking.

"Don't touch me," she cried. "I don't want your pity or your kindness."

He was at a loss for words, but he wrapped his arms around her, squeezing her even more tightly against him. "Amber," he began gently, "I never meant to hurt you. I only wanted to protect you."

"Why do I feel so wretched, then?"

"It's all my fault," he murmured with a self-deprecating grin. "The role of knight in shining armor is a new one for me. I'm a bit clumsy."

"Oh, Jake, I don't want some knight in shining armor with high-minded ideals about me. I'm not that kind of girl. I'm not sure I even deserve your respect."

"I'm sure."

"Kiss me again," she begged, not understanding her bold behavior any more than he understood his reticence. "I can't stand it." Never had she so blatantly pursued a man. "Please, Jake... I'm dying for you."

"I'm dying for you, too."

She could feel his heart hammering against his rib cage. Some instinct drove her to touch him, to lift her fingertips to his mouth, to trace its firm, warm outline.

He shuddered at her touch, and she was conscious of a vague sensation of triumph. At least he was not immune to her.

"Amber—" His harsh tone warned her. He removed her hand. "Before, I wanted you the way I've wanted other women. Now you're special to me. I don't want to rush you. I want you to accept me as a person before you accept me as a lover. I fell in love once before, and I made a mess of things. I don't want to make the same mistakes again."

She stared at him in wonder. His dark face was grave. There was an intensity about him she didn't understand. She realized with a start that her own feelings were equally intense, and that she didn't know what they meant either.

Oh, she should push him away. For his own sake she shouldn't let him become more deeply involved with her. And yet...

She felt so safe in his arms. When she remembered the terror of the afternoon, she knew that she was afraid to go on fighting her battles alone. She needed him, and even though she would be surrendering to her old weakness, she knew that it was no longer in her to deny the need she felt for him.

He led her outside to the porch. The sky was a blaze of vivid desert pinks with shadings of purple. Over the mountains a rainbow arced.

He clasped her hand tightly in his, as if afraid she would run if he let her go. He looked at her. In the reddish gold light her tear-streaked face seemed softly flushed. Her mussed hair was a shower of flame.

The beauty of her seemed to spread through him, into his bones and deep into his body, and he hated the things he had to say. He wanted to prolong this magic moment of silence.

He expelled a soft sigh. "Don't you think it's about time you leveled with me?" he whispered at last.

"About what?"

"The trouble you're in."

"How—" The color in her cheeks heightened, and she twisted her hand nervously in his, trying to pull it free. "I mean, what in the world are you talking about, Jake?"

He held on to her hand and pulled her closer. "Amber, who was that man this afternoon?"

She couldn't quite meet his eyes. "I told you."

"Everything but the truth," he replied quietly.

"I don't want to discuss him."

"That man was a professional. What in the hell does he want with you?"

"I—I can't say," Amber stammered, and her eyes fell again before his candid regard.

"Tell me then, why did you come to live with Hamlin in the first place?"

"I—I just came. Does there have to be a reason?"

He measured her with cool green eyes. "Yes."

"Jake, you have no right to pry."

"Amber, I know you're running from something, and I know you're afraid. I want to help you."

"Jake, this is something I have to work out for myself."

"You're too independent." There was warmth in his voice, and pride. And she deserved neither.

If he only knew.

"It's odd. Amber, I find your determination to solve your own problems very appealing, and yet at the same time the chauvinist in me wants to make things easier for you."

And she wanted him to. Oh, she wanted him to. How easy it would be if only she could shove all her problems on his wide shoulders. But what would he think of her if he knew the truth? Wouldn't his admiration turn to disgust?

She felt a sudden tearing pain, and she knew she couldn't bear it if he despised her for what she'd done.

"Hold me, Jake," she whispered. "Just hold me. Don't let me go. Ever."

Chapter Ten

Amber's hand shook as she carefully wrote a check to Don for several thousand dollars. It would deplete almost all of her savings, but she wouldn't think about that. All that mattered was Don, and what those men might do to him if she didn't send him the money.

Quickly she stuffed the check into an envelope and slipped it into her purse, as if it were something evil and frightening and she wanted it out of her sight.

On her work table, the silver bracelet she'd been working on caught the light. She picked it up, her troubled expression vanishing, a smile of quiet pride touching her lips.

Her skill had grown. Never had she dreamed she could have made so much money, so quickly. For once in her life she'd succeeded at something all by herself.

She set the bracelet down and went back to work, determined to craft more jewelry, to make more money, and to dig her way out of the terrible mess she'd made of her life.

That morning she'd gotten up early so she could get a few hours of jewelry-making in before she took time off to run errands. Serena had tried to be understanding about the damage done to her Corvette, and Amber was determined not only to pay for whatever the insurance didn't cover, but to take it into Denver for repairs herself so that Serena would not be bothered. While she was in Denver, Amber planned to mail the check to Don.

A little chill went through her as she remembered the man with the pale eyes and the damp smile, a slow dread seeping into her body as she recalled how he'd effortlessly pressed her elbow and produced such nerve-splintering pain, how he'd smiled when he'd inflicted that torture.

Her pulse throbbed unevenly, and she prayed that the money would keep him satisfied, at least for a while.

It was already well past noon when the sound of a car in the drive distracted her from setting an amethyst in a golden ring. Flicking the miniblinds apart, she recognized the familiar blue truck. Jake got out, and strode up the drive toward the house.

Her interest in the ring died. Her eyes fell indifferently to the glimmering stone, and she realized it would be pointless to work longer.

The minute she stepped inside the dark stillness of the ranch house, she caught the sound of hushed voices coming from the library.

There was something mysterious about those murmuring voices. Something vaguely alarming. They could only belong to Jake and Serena. Paula had not come in to work yet, and Hamlin was outside working with the animals. David was at school. But why had Jake sought out Serena?

Curious, Amber went to the polished pecan doors and raised the cool brass handles. As the library doors parted she discovered Jake and Serena standing in a pool of sunshine streaming through the long windows, having an intense, and very private, conversation.

Their dark heads were together. There seemed a closeness, a rightness about them somehow, and suddenly Amber wished she'd never come into the house and found them.

The moment they became aware of her they jumped apart and stopped talking. For a second, Serena's eyes were wild, as if she'd been discovered and felt guilty.

Amber remembered her previous doubts concerning Serena and Jake. Had they been lovers? Were they still?

No! She was overreacting! They were just old friends. Everything was exactly the way Serena had explained it.

Amber's throat felt dry. She swallowed, but it did no good. Oh, why had she barged in on them? She wanted to leave, but she couldn't. She hung there in the doorway, her stomach twisting.

"Oh, hi there, Amber," Jake said, a little too smoothly, after an infinitesimal pause. "I was on my way to find you."

"You were?" Amber's disbelieving question seemed to hang in the air. A multitude of unasked questions hung there too.

"To see if you'd like to drive into Denver with me for dinner and a play tonight."

Serena wouldn't look up from the dead cigarette she was squashing in a Waterford ashtray.

"Th-that would be wonderful, Jake," Amber managed falteringly, struggling to make her voice light and casual, and failing abysmally. "I—I was going to take Serena's car to a garage in Denver. Maybe you wouldn't mind following behind, and we could ride home together. I was sort of afraid I might have trouble on the road."

"It would be my pleasure."

He crossed the room and placed his hands on her shoulders. His fingers were warm, electric. In that moment she felt very silly for all her little fears.

"How's the shoulder?" he asked.

"Much better."

"You're looking very beautiful today, Amber," he said softly, folding her into his arms.

Serena made some sound and hurried from the room.

"I—I didn't mean to interrupt you and Serena, Jake," Amber said.

"You didn't."

"You seemed . . . engrossed."

"It wasn't important."

But there was something in his eyes that made her wonder.

Jake took Amber to his favorite Chinese restaurant in Denver, at the top of a skyscraper. Jake ordered drinks before dinner, and they took forever to come.

The restaurant was dark and handsome, with lots of red lacquer and sparkling Chinese lanterns. Below, the city was a carpet of twinkling lights.

"The view is wonderful," Amber murmured delightedly as she sank deeper in the thick red leather cushions. She removed her white sweater, and primly folded her hands together on top of the glossy black table.

"It certainly is," he replied. He was looking at her, admiring the low-cut white dress that revealed the smoothness of her shoulders and the flawless curves of her breasts.

"Jake," she chided, "you're not even looking at the mountains."

"No," he agreed lazily, his gaze lingering on the voluptuous swells of peach skin above the plunging neckline. "My view is much lovelier."

She blushed. His eyes seemed to burn her. "I want to know what they all are."

"What?"

"The mountains, Jake."

"Ah, yes, the mountains..." Reluctantly he turned his attention to the windows. "That's Long's Peak over there. It's fifty miles away in Rocky Mountain National Park. Toward the west, that's Mount Evans."

"You must love the mountains," she said, "to have come back to them."

"I can tell you're in the mood to hear the story of my life." He smiled at her, that irresistible, slightly mocking smile of his that made her feel warm and tingly.

"Yes," she murmured. "Tell me all your dark secrets."

Her blue eyes gazed steadily at him. He stared back at her.

"What man could resist an invitation like that?" He grinned and his eyes danced with amusement. "Well, since you asked, my mountaineering began in my boyhood. I used to look out my schoolroom window at those very same mountains. Later there were the mountain-climbing trips with my father, before he died."

She listened spellbound, feeling a funny little sense of loss, remembering how as a child she was forever longing for her mother to do things with her, to take her places. But her mother never had.

"Dad and I would climb all day, until we were dead tired. Then we'd pitch camp. He used to make me beef-and-bacon squares impaled on a long spit, and toast, and marshmallows, all over a great open fire. The stars would be so bright you felt like you could reach out and touch them. I loved the animals. Sometimes we'd see bighorn springing noiselessly up some headwall. There were mountain jays, marmots, beavers. Lots of others, too. Sometimes it would snow. Sometimes we'd get to the top of one mountain, and as we'd come over the shoulder we'd see other peaks gleaming in rows beyond them. I wanted to climb every one of them. To me the mountains were heaven, a kind of exhilarating freedom, and I never wanted to come down."

"I can imagine."

"Maybe I liked the mountains because there were things I wanted to run away from. People didn't think all that much of my father." Jake's voice had deepened subtly. His amusement had vanished. "But he was my hero. He was a family man, and he didn't make friends easily. He never made much money, either. There were times when he drank too much, but he was quiet when he did that, like he was eaten up by some private unhappiness he couldn't tell anybody about. There were times I was ashamed of him because he didn't make more of a success of life. Then I would hate myself for those feelings. He never abused his family. I was twelve when he died, and for a while I thought my world had come to an end."

"You were lucky," she said wistfully, "to have had him at all."

"I know that now, and that's why it hurt like hell losing him."

"There are lots of ways to get hurt, Jake."

He looked at her quizzically, his eyes kind. "Why don't you tell me about yourself?"

She toyed with a spoon on the table. "Oh, there's nothing to tell, really."

"Why do women with fascinating pasts always say that? The ones with perfectly ordinary lives talk all night."

She knew the answer to that. There were wounds that went so deep they couldn't heal. Wounds that still hurt every time she remembered. There was the fear that if he knew the truth he wouldn't want her.

"To me you're a woman of mystery. You came to my valley for reasons unknown, and I know nothing of your life before. But my life's an open book. Serena tosses you a few pages from time to time. You have only to ask Paula to learn more. You could call up my business partners and find out what a scramble I'm having coming up with the money I owe every month. There's nothing you can't discover about me."

"I have no intention of prying into your past or your present, Jake."

Again he grinned, sheepishly, charmingly. "I guess you're different from all the other women I've known, then."

Only because she had something to hide.

Amber tossed her head lightly, and the last rays of the setting sun made threads of fire of her hair. Her eyes were softly luminous, vulnerable. "Why don't we dance."

She felt his hand cover hers, and she gave an audible little sigh. He helped her out of her chair, led her to the dance floor and wrapped her in his arms.

The music was soft and melodious. The sky was rapidly darkening, turning from blue to a rich deep purple. The moon had just risen.

They were the only couple on the dance floor, and it was wonderful dancing in the moonlight, smothered tightly in his arms, pressed into that hard masculine body. Nothing mattered but the ecstasy of being held by him. Don was forgotten, and the mess she'd made of her life seemed inconsequential.

Later, when they returned to their table, the ice had melted in their drinks. They had a marvelous dinner. He ordered crispy duck, and she had scallops with garlic sauce. They lingered over the meal, the wine, the dessert. And each other.

The candle on their table burned low as they talked for hours. They never made it to the play. He took her to a nightclub overlooking a glimmering lake, where they danced until she was exhausted.

Then he drove her back to the ranch at a speed that seemed no speed at all, the lights whipping by in the velvet blackness like brilliant bullets. She fell asleep with his arm around her, and only he was left awake to contemplate the marvel of the evening they had just spent together.

From time to time his eyes left the road, and he studied the bright head resting so trustingly against his shoulder. After a time she sighed contentedly in her sleep and shifted, her head falling lower. He eased it still further downward, to his thigh. Her hair spilled between his legs. She murmured something unintelligible in a little breathy voice. Her hand moved to his lap, her fingers clutching fabric and curling against the hard warmth of muscle.

At this little movement, he sucked in a quick, hoarse breath and clenched the steering wheel. Then he cursed, half aloud, half to himself. The slender fingers moved again, and he bit into his lip.

When he began to sweat, he yanked his tie loose and jerkily unbuttoned his collar. The truck cab seemed stifling, but when he rolled the window down a little he was instantly cold and shaking.

He wanted to pull the truck to the shoulder and take her then and there.

What in the hell was wrong with him? It was as if he were a green kid who hadn't yet taken his first woman. He felt ridiculous. He was used to being in control, not panting like some adolescent. What had happened to his casual approach toward women and sex? Didn't he have enough problems of his own at the moment? The last thing he needed was to become deeply involved with this woman. Hell, one would have thought he had learned his lesson. Why couldn't he seem to stop himself, then, from caring far too much?

It was as if he had become a different man, and he no longer knew himself.

He caught the scent of her perfume. There was a subtle sweetness to it as it enveloped him. It seemed to seep inside him, to possess him, as the woman possessed him.

The road seemed endless. It was torture. His callused palm touched the silken masses of her hair. It was ecstasy.

She awakened only when they arrived at the ranch. When he gently touched her shoulder, and she looked into his darkly handsome face, she felt that she was in a dream. She tried to close her eyes again, telling him that she was too happy, that she never wanted to wake up, that she didn't want to go inside, that she wanted to stay in his arms forever.

Hadn't she always been a creature of dreams?

She had no idea how voluptuous he thought her, how sensually tantalizing. He was almost afraid to touch her again because he wanted to so fiercely.

Tenderly he shook her awake again, promising to take her into the mountains the next day.

He let her out of the cab and she ran inside, her white dress fluttering in the moonlight, her shimmering hair falling back over her shoulders.

He hadn't kissed her, and yet the silent, unspoken longing in his eyes had told her how much he wanted her.

It had been the most erotic evening of her life.

And she had fallen irrevocably, devastatingly in love.

He came for her at noon, after making a brief trip that morning to Steamboat Springs to talk with his contractor. She was ready and waiting for him, dressed in skin-tight blue jeans and a tight green sweater. When she saw his truck, she ran breathlessly out to meet him.

He leaned across the seat and opened the door for her. Capturing her hand in his, he helped her inside.

For a long moment they just sat together, each savoring the exquisite stillness of the other, the intense pleasure of being together once again, the smoldering awkwardness that comes when lovers don't dare touch. Then, just when she thought he might kiss her, he leaned forward and started the truck.

A little sigh of disappointment escaped her lips, and though she knew he would have preferred that she stay where she was, she moved across the seat to sit beside him.

Almost reluctantly, his arm encircled her shoulder and he drew her closer. Though his hand rested lightly on her shoulder, she could feel his fingertips, burning hot, through her soft wool sweater.

They drove in silence, but she was not unaware of him. She was in love, and she was afraid of loving. Falling in love was like climbing a mountain. The higher one climbed, the more tragically dangerous could be the fall.

It was a bright sunny afternoon, but as the truck climbed into the mountains there was a slight frost in the air that glazed the red sandstone and sparkled on the grasses. There was a thin layer of snow coating the distant peaks. The day seemed magic, painfully wonderful, because she was with Jake, and she felt a little foolish to be so gloriously happy.

The road curved up the mountain, weaving around boulders, through groves of aspen and sweet-smelling pine. From time to time sparkling streams trickled down the mountainside.

Jake maneuvered the truck with skillful ease.

"It's all so gorgeous," Amber said, breaking the silence between them at last, not really knowing what to say, but wanting to say something just so he would be compelled to answer and she could listen to the deep rhythm of his voice.

"It makes me wish I knew something about geology."

His fingers tightened on her shoulder. "I could give you quite a lecture, if you're really in the mood."

"Oh, I am," she teased.

"It's really quite simple. You see, for a mere half-a-billion years this land was repeatedly warped and broken by cataclysmic forces like erosion. It was flooded by intruding seas."

"Jake!" She was laughing gently. "You really are going to give me a lecture."

"You asked for it, darling."

He had called her "darling." She was only half-listening after that, savoring the casually tossed endearment.

"Then only a mere eighty million years ago—that's roughly a weekend to geologists, my love—we had something called the Laramide Revolution that shaped today's Rockies. The crust of Colorado was lifted up. Volcanoes belched and molten rock seeped into crevices. When the fluid fire cooled, some of it crystallized into mineral veins and lodes that gave men some pretty compelling reasons to come to Colorado."

"It all sounds so wildly dramatic, so passionate," she murmured.

"A little like the way you make me feel," came the deep, quiet drawl.

Then there was the stillness again, more intense than ever before. The breathless tension hovered between them, a terrible, unspoken wanting.

He removed his arm from her shoulder. They lapsed into silence, afraid to talk, afraid to touch.

They were surrounded by golden aspens. Every leaf was doing a shimmering dance in the breeze. Each a sparkling golden droplet, quivering, making its special dry rustling sound. Beneath the trees the ground was carpeted with the brightness of fallen leaves.

"They're so beautiful," she murmured. "What makes them tremble all the time?"

"Well, the Utes, the Indians who used to live around here, have an old legend about that. They say that the Great Spirit once planned a special visit to earth during a full moon. All the forest creatures began to tremble at this sacred honor. But the proud aspen would not pay tribute, and stood quite still, unawed by the Great Spirit's coming. Well, the Great Spirit got very angry and declared that forever after, the leaves of the aspen would tremble when anyone looked upon it."

"Oh, Jake, that's lovely."

A few miles further, Jake parked the truck, and Amber slid quickly across the seat, opened her own door, and hopped out onto the red gravel road. The air was cold and brisk, and she reached in her pockets and pulled on her gloves. She made a show of being busy as she went to the back of the pickup and pulled out her backpack, adjusting straps, checking to make sure everything was packed securely.

"This is where we walk," he said, after he'd gathered his own equipment.

"Up the road?"

"Up the mountain." He pointed toward two ruts that wound steeply upward through the tress. She thought she detected a hint of laughter in his voice as he helped her put on her backpack.

"Straight up?" she muttered, and then was furious with herself for it.

"Don't worry, you have only to say the word and we'll turn back." Fleetingly his eyes touched hers with their warmth.

They stepped over a fallen log and began to walk up the rough road. Jake told her it was an old gold-mine road. The road had long ago been forgotten, and spruces as high as a man grew between the ruts.

All too soon Amber was breathless. She felt like collapsing, but he made her keep going. When they finally stopped so she could rest, he went into the forest and found a tall stick she could use to help her with the climb.

"I'm not sure I'm going to be able to keep up with you," she said.

"It's always hard at first."

There was no wind where they were, only a deep green-and-gold silence, but they could hear the wind sighing beneath them. They could watch it gently ruffle the tops of the trees as it whispered through them, and they could hear the faint dry rustlings of the aspens.

Jake was right. The hike did get easier, and as they climbed higher the scenery became more spectacular.

They ate their lunch by a lake, watching a beaver colony trail their shimmering wakes behind them in the brilliant water.

They came to a lonely mine shack, bleached to silver by high storms, now abandoned. Beyond it there was a magnificent view and the mountains seemed to stretch away forever in an endless ruffling of cold white peaks.

"I used to come here with my father," he said quietly, pulling her into his arms. "I wanted you to see all this."

For a long while she stood there staring at the mountains while he looked at her. The wind caught her hair and swirled it.

"All my life, I'll remember this moment," he said.

Very gently he kissed her lips, a long, tender, undemanding kiss. After it was over, he held her tightly to him, and it seemed to her that they were the only man and the only woman ever to know such rapture.

Before her, as if thrown down in a rumpled snowy carpet, was the majestic splendor of those glistening mountains, but Jake was splendor too.

After a long time he took her hand and led her a little farther up the trail, until they came to an abandoned mine. There was a crumbling building. Ore buckets still hung on a rusting cable that swept upward, from the top-floor window to the canyon wall in a thousand-foot parabola. At its high end and along the rimrock, they could see tiny holes where men had gone up with their donkeys or in the ore buckets to do a day's work.

"Oh, Jake, imagine living up here for months on end, cut off from the world."

"I'm not sure I'd mind, if I had you." He drew her fully against him. His arms came around her, pressing her to the long, hard length of him. Her own arms locked around his neck.

"I never dreamed I could feel like this again," he said softly. Then he pressed his lips shudderingly against her throat. He was trembling, and so was she. She closed her eyes, waiting for his kisses to deepen, waiting for him to lose control, longing for him to take her.

But he didn't deepen his kisses. Instead, he gave her a final kiss that was infinitely tender, and continued to hold her, his hands gently caressing her until his ragged breathing subsided. Then he told her it was time they went back down the mountain.

All too soon the wonderful day was nearly over, and they were sitting in a roadside café, having supper, holding hands across a red and white checkered tablecloth. Earlier, they had laughed together over the western decor—unvarnished pine flooring, stone walls covered with faded paintings of cowboys and Indians, saddles and stirrups hanging from varnished rafters. Their waitress was a pretty Indian girl with thick black braids and a straw cowboy hat.

"I feel like I walked into a wild-West movie set," Amber had said.

"This place is wild, all right. A bit overdone."

Later, when they were eating charred steaks from sizzling metal platters, the front door flew open and Amber glanced up, almost expecting a ferocious gunslinger to stride menacingly into the café. Instead a short dark man with a sunburned face and worried blue eyes stepped meekly inside. He glanced quickly around the room, and when he spotted Jake, he beckoned him with an apologetic wave. Amber felt Jake's fingers press more tightly into hers, and he frowned in recognition before nodding toward the man. Under his breath he said, "Excuse me for a minute, Amber. That's my builder. It must be damned important, or Billy wouldn't have come looking for me."

Without bothering to introduce her, Jake led the stranger outside where they could talk privately. Amber waited, toying with her food rather than eating it, sensing trouble and upset that Jake's steak was getting cold while he was away.

When Jake returned, he didn't reach for her hand. Instead, he ate in deadly silence. Nor was he in the mood to listen to her when she tried to distract him with light chatter. When she broke off finally, in the middle of a sentence, it seemed as if he didn't even notice.

He was only half finished with his steak when he dropped his knife and fork on the plate with a clatter. He pushed the platter aside and reached for the bill. Her hand closed over his.

"You're not going to tell me what's wrong, are you?" she ventured.

He gave her a quick, freezing look that was meant to silence her. Very carefully, he removed her hand. Then he pulled out his wallet and counted crisp green bills.

"Jake, what's wrong?"

"Look, Amber, I think I'd better just take you home."

"I know that man must have given you some upsetting news. It might help if you talked about it."

Jade-green eyes froze her. "How would you know? You wouldn't come running to me and confide, now, would you, if you had a problem?"

"Jake, that's not fair."

"It's only the truth," came his terse answer.

They were in the truck. Doors slammed. Seat buckles snapped. No glances. No words. Only an awkward awareness of the silence between them as he turned the key in the ignition.

It had showered while they were in the café, and the pavement was wet. The street lamps glowed in the lingering mist like great ripe oranges, and there were golden glimmerings in the gutters.

The truck swept past the gaily lit shops that lined the main street of the ski resort, boutiques selling fashionable ski clothing, a bakery that gave off the aroma of new bread. From a brightly lit bar filled with logging crews came the low, compelling drumbeat of rock music and the sound of men's laughter.

The lights of the last house vanished, and the truck plunged into the hills and the thick black night. Jake was driving fast, and though he always drove fast, there was a difference in the way he was handling the truck tonight. He drove with a vengeance, as though he were determined to take out all his frustrations on the road. He was pushing himself—his skill, the truck, and Amber—to the edge.

For a while, Amber stared into the rushing darkness, nails digging into her palms. She watched breathlessly as the truck ate up the blue road. He took a turn too fast, and she had to grab for her purse to keep it from sliding onto the floorboard. Her fingers clenched so tightly around the plastic handles that they hurt.

He took another turn, faster than the one before. The handles of her purse were cold knives cutting into her fingertips.

She stole a worried glance toward Jake's silent profile. Gone was the man of warmth and charm who only the night before had talked of his boyhood, who'd romanced her so tenderly as they'd dance for hours in the nightclub beside that glistening lake. Beside her now was a furious, dark stranger intent upon his driving, totally absorbed in his own thoughts; he had forgotten she was even there.

Tires screamed as he recklessly took a third turn that wound down to a narrow bridge, and Amber felt a little sick to her stomach.

"Jake, please." Her voice was a hushed sound in the silence of the cab. "You're scaring me."

His only response was to lift his foot fractionally from the accelerator. She felt the truck slowing, though only a little.

He had bought a pack of cigarettes from the restaurant cashier. He ripped the pack from his shirt pocket, tore into the cellophane, tossed the garbage onto the floor and lit a cigarette with the truck's lighter. He inhaled deeply, silently. Then he opened his window a crack.

"I've never seen you smoke before," she said, thinking maybe she was wrong to let him dominate them both with this black, terrible silence.

"I quit over a year ago."

"You must be very worried."

"I am."

"Tell me."

"That's not something either one of us is particularly good at, confessing that we've got a problem maybe we can't handle."

"Jake—"

"Just forget it, okay? I'll work it out," he said in the low, grudging tone she hated.

"You're determined to shut me out, aren't you? I don't mean anything to you, then. Not really."

"Hell!" he said between his teeth.

And that was all either of them said until they reached the ranch.

He drove more slowly after that, but somehow his doing so seemed a careful insult, as if his anger were now directed solely at her.

When he stopped the truck in front of the ranch house, he cut the motor. They sat in strained silence, and the tension between them ate away at Amber. She curled her lip between her teeth, hesitating, wishing she could think of something to say. Nothing came to mind.

She was aware of him staring at her, and she turned, wishing there was some way she could reach him.

Silver moonlight illuminated her pale face. The soft light was lambent in her wide eyes; his were narrowed and cool, raking her. Not by the flicker of an eyelid did he reveal that her pain disturbed him.

He lit another cigarette and then jammed it into the ashtray. A wisp of smoke curled away, dying, leaving only a lingering, faintly acrid scent.

She started to reach out to him, but her hand dropped back into her lap, where it lay frozen and white, helpless. She didn't know what to say, what to do, and she hated herself because she felt so inadequate.

After a while she grasped the cold door handle. "Goodnight, Jake," she whispered, lifting the handle. And then, recklessly, because he seemed so indifferent, because she felt so close to tears and wanted to hurt him, "It's obvious you don't care whether I go or stay."

"Don't care—" His savage voice was a low throb that seemed to strangle him and prevent further speech.

She opened the door and was about to jump out when he gripped her upper arm and jerked her roughly toward him. She tried to fight him, but he only turned her swiftly in his arms and lowered his head, forcing her to accept the brutal assault of his mouth.

His kiss was harsh and angry. He crushed her body beneath his; she felt the wild hammering of his heartbeats, the hoarse breath that felt torn from his lungs. Amber was breathless too, and shaking; her body racked by long, fearful shudders. But she returned his kiss with more passion than she had ever felt before.

As quickly as he'd taken her, he let her go, and she fell back against the seat, totally shaken by the volcanic emotion in his kiss. She tried to tell herself that she was furious at him for treating her so brutally, that it wasn't a new and terribly unsettling kind of passion she felt.

"I care, damn you," he finally said. "More than I should, and more than I want to."

He opened his door, and was about to come around to let her out, but she didn't wait. She jumped out of the truck, slammed the door and ran toward the house.

"Amber!"

She ignored him, or rather she ran all the faster when he called after her.

Jake watched her hurl herself frantically up the steps, nearly falling. He watched as she switched on the porch lights and fumbled furiously in her purse for the key. He watched until she vanished inside, and the porch was dark once more.

He got back in the cab and lit another cigarette. Upstairs, a bedroom light came on, and he wondered if it was hers. A while later he watched the light go out. He smoked another cigarette, and another.

He should go. There was no reason he should stay. No reason... The thought trailed away.

He didn't need her. There was no room in his life for more trouble. And she was trouble. Every time he remembered the man who'd been after her, Jake knew he had no business getting involved with her. They weren't going to do one another any good, that was certain. But he couldn't help himself.

He couldn't get her touch, her smell, the heat of her body out of his mind.

"Damn."

He got out of the truck and threw the cigarette on the drive, grinding it out with the heel of his boot. He reached inside the cab and grabbed the backpack she'd forgotten from behind the seat. Then he stalked up to the house and rang the bell.

Chapter Eleven

Serena opened the door, and Jake caught the faint scent of wild roses. Her eyebrows arched in surprise when she saw him and her lips curved in a cool smile that was slightly mocking.

A smile Jake didn't return.

Serena's dark curls were brushed away from her face and held by golden butterfly clips, her hair gleaming in the subdued light from the chandelier. She was casually elegant in a lavender jump suit. On each arm she wore bands of golden Gypsy circlets that jingled faintly every time she moved. She was beautiful and she knew it.

The wildness in her eyes sent a message he didn't want to accept. He tore his eyes from her lovely face. From the pain. From the memories. "I want to see Amber," he muttered thickly.

"Maybe she doesn't want to see you." Serena's velvet voice was faintly accusing.

"Maybe not, but she will."

"You're always so sure of yourself these days, aren't you, Jake Kassidy? There was a time, not so long ago, when you weren't so cocky."

His mouth twisted bitterly. "I remember that time a hell of a lot better than you do."

"I liked you better back then."

"Did you, Serena? Sometimes I wonder."

"There are some that say you may be coming on hard times again, Jake."

"And I bet that would make you real happy, wouldn't it, Serena? To see me down again where you thought I belonged. Where you wanted me to stay because then you would never have suffered one moment of regret for the way you..." He stopped himself. "That's past history, and I don't give a damn about it anymore."

Something awful and vulnerable had come into her eyes. Something he didn't want to acknowledge.

"Where in the hell's Hamlin?" Jake growled.

"He's out of town."

"I see. So you're feeling lonely?"

"J—Jake..."

"I came to see Amber," he said softly. "She forgot her backpack." It thudded heavily as he set it on the floor.

"I'll give it to her."

"No. I'm not leaving until I see her."

He started to step past Serena.

"Jake! You can't just barge in here like you own the place. This is my home."

"And Hamlin's," he jeered softly. "Why is it always so easy for you to forget about him?"

"And Hamlin's," she whispered.

"If you don't get Amber down for me fast, I'll go up after her myself."

"Jake, you're behaving like a maniac."

"Maybe that's because I'm starting to feel like one. Go get her, Serena. You'll save us both a lot of time."

"Wait here," she said icily.

It was nearly ten minutes before Serena reappeared with Amber.

Beside the glamorous Serena, Amber looked like a pale, lost child. She wore a white terry robe that was too long for her, and her face had been scrubbed free of makeup. Her huge glasses were perched a little crookedly on the slender bridge of her nose, but even though they were tinted he could see that her eyes were red. She'd been crying. Because of him.

And because she looked so very young, almost like a frightened little girl, Jake suddenly felt like a heel.

Serena started to leave them, but Amber's thready whisper stopped her.

"Don't leave me alone with him."

At that, Jake's feelings of guilt grew stronger than ever. Serena paused, uncertain, and he nodded toward her to stay.

"You forgot your backpack," Jake said inconsequentially to Amber.

"I know," came the taut, frozen whisper that cut through his gut. He'd scared her and upset her, and he didn't like himself very much.

"I thought maybe you might need it," he said.

"Thank you for bringing it back."

"Hell! Amber..." Why couldn't he think of anything to say to her?

"Jake..." she whispered.

And suddenly he didn't need to think of the right words, because the right feelings were there. She was hesitant at first, but then she was flying across the room into his arms, and he was cradling her flushed face in his hands, removing her glasses, gently kissing the top of her head, then her brows, her nose, her cheeks. Her lips. He drank of her. Lost himself in her sweetness.

Why had he cut himself off from her—even for a second?

Serena vanished from the room, and neither of them noticed.

"Sometimes I hate you, Jake Kassidy."

"Sometimes I hate you, too," he told her.

"But not right now?" she said.

"No..." His smile was gentle. He pulled her to him and pressed her body into his, almost hurting her, kissing her more passionately than he'd ever kissed any woman.

At last he said, in an odd breathless voice, "The way I figure it, I'm going to have to be gone for at least a week to Denver and Steamboat Springs on business, but when I come back next Friday, would you come to my house for dinner? I'll barbecue steaks. Maybe you can help me toss a salad. We won't go anywhere special. We'll just be together."

She read between the lines. He wasn't going to tell her what was wrong, at least not now, but he was telling her that he was going to make love to her.

She didn't hesitate. "Yes, I'll come."

Her eyes promised him much more.

He kissed her again, and they held on to each other for a long time. Then he finally said goodbye and left her standing there, watching after him long after his truck had vanished into the darkness.

Amber was halfway up the stairs, floating away in a dream, when Serena's hoarse whisper broke into her pleasant reverie. "Amber, would you mind coming back down?"

The dream was instantly shattered, and Amber realized she was exhausted from the long hike and the quarrel she'd had with Jake.

"Serena," she said wearily, sagging against the bannister, "it's been a long day, and I'm very tired. I'm afraid I don't feel much like talking."

"I can imagine, darling," the cool voice taunted her. "But this will only take a moment."

Amber reluctantly followed Serena into the den. Serena must have been watching television while Jake was there, because the set was on with the sound turned down. The ashtray beside the chair was filled with spent cigarettes. The den smelled of smoke.

Serena lit a cigarette. Amber had the impression of a caged cat that couldn't be still. Serena picked up a magazine that had fallen onto the carpet and replaced it on the end table. Then she moved a lamp to the center of its end table and straightened the shade. Her fingers were shaking slightly, and Amber watched her with growing dread. At last Serena found the courage to launch into her topic.

"Amber, you know I want you to date and have fun."

Some fleeting surprise must have shown in Amber's face, because Serena felt the need to be more emphatic. "Surely you remember that I practically had to push you out of the house when you first came here."

"Yes, I remember."

"I've told you before that I would give anything if you would find someone else to go out with besides Jake."

Amber was silent for a moment. "I tried, Serena, but now there's no one else I want to date."

"Amber darling, that just can't be true!"

"I'm afraid it is. You're going to have to try to get over your past differences with Jake."

A pause. "It's not that I don't like Jake," Serena said carefully. "I just don't want him in my house. Around you. I wish him well. Believe me. As long as he stays a long way away."

"Why do you feel that way about him?"

There was a short silence, and Serena stubbed out her cigarette. Her hands were clasped together, white in the faint glow from the television. "Just take my word that he's using you, Amber darling. I know him better than you do. We grew up together."

In a voice as thin as a thread, Amber said, "Maybe you knew him then; I'm not so sure you know him now."

Serena made a small strangled sound. "Damn it, I'm trying to help you. Why won't you believe me?"

Briefly, Amber met her fierce gaze; then both women looked away.

Amber scraped her nails against her dry, ice-cold palms. "I can't stop seeing Jake."

Serena's whisper was desperate, needle-sharp. "You're in love with him, aren't you?"

Amber nodded silently, wretchedly. A pulse knocked even in her fingertips as she watched Serena whirl away and run to the window, where she stood looking out though it was impossible to see in the darkness. "Oh, Amber, darling. This can't be happening. I won't let it happen."

"There's nothing you can do to stop it."

"Oh, isn't there?"

Amber was about to say something, but as she struggled to frame her response, the telephone beside her rang jarringly. She picked it up on the first ring, almost glad of the interruption.

"Hello?" she said, half hoping it would be Jake.

There was only silence. Only Serena staring at her from across the room with that terrible haunted look on her white face, with her too-brilliant eyes. Only Amber's own pulse, suddenly slamming against her rib cage in a horrified rush.

"Who is it?" Amber said, her voice no more than a terrified breath. "Tell me who you are."

A whisper said, "The money you sent wasn't enough."

Amber's heart jerked in a violent spasm of fear. On a sharply rising note she cried, "It has to be."

The line went dead.

The telephone dropped from her trembling fingers to the floor. She made a strangled sound that might have been a sob.

She couldn't stand it if that man came after her again. If he took her away. She remembered how easily he'd hurt her. How it had given him pleasure to do so.

What would he do to her if he came back?

Fear flicked through her shaking body like a whip.

She wanted Jake. In that moment she would have told him everything.

She scarcely noticed Serena coming quietly across the room and picking up the dangling telephone.

Amber's heart kept beating in those sharp, hammering little strokes. Before Serena could say anything, Amber turned and fled the room.

She locked her bedroom door and threw herself across the bed.

Every time she started to call Jake she told herself that in the morning she would feel better, that this was not his problem. It was something she had to handle alone.

Jake was driving fast. Plumes of pink dust boiled behind the truck as he headed across the last stretch of road toward his ranch house. He knew he should slow down, but he was anxious to get home after his week away, anxious to call Amber, anxious to put behind him everything he'd been through this past week.

If only he could.

He felt like he'd been through a meat grinder. Ever since his partner had told him he wanted to default on the note, Jake's finances had been in jeopardy. Unless he obtained a new partner or new financing, his negative monthly cash flow would force him to shut down.

What he needed was a cold beer, a hot shower, and Amber, and not necessarily in that order.

A year ago he couldn't do anything wrong. Now he couldn't do anything right. His money problems with the resort seemed to be compounding, but since he'd already poured the foundations and started construction, it was too late to back out.

With hard times hitting the oil industry, investors in Texas, Colorado and Oklahoma were drying up faster than water holes in a drought. He'd gone to every banker he knew, begging for more money and more time. He wondered if he'd accomplished anything in Denver.

He stopped in front of the house, deciding not to put the truck in the garage until after he called Amber. Lifting his suitcase and briefcase out of the truck, he walked toward his house, the jacket of his suit slung over one shoulder. On the porch, he set his briefcase down and reached for his key. Then he noticed the door was ajar.

Pete, the hired hand, must have forgotten to lock up. Jake pushed the door open and stepped inside. It was dark in the house after the brilliance of the desert, and it took his eyes a moment to grow accustomed to the dimness.

He caught the scent of wild roses, fragrant and elusive, as it mingled with the acrid smell of a burning cigarette. Only one woman smelled of those things.

Serena was curled on his recliner, dressed in tight black jeans and a black silk shirt. She was drinking her second imported beer.

His imported beer.

She leaned back, and a ray of golden sunlight streamed over her body and backlighted her hair.

She was beautiful. More beautiful than ever.

Deliberately beautiful, he thought, yet he felt no desire for her as he once would have.

"I'd offer you a drink, but I see you already have one. What are you doing here, anyway?" he asked in a bland, cool tone.

"When you first came back, you told me where the key was and that I was welcome anytime," she replied huskily. "Remember?"

Oh, he remembered. Though he would have preferred not to. He'd made one hell of a fool of himself that day.

"It took you a while to take me up on my invitation," he replied dryly, not looking at her.

"Well, I'm here now."

"Alone at last." He laughed, but it was a rueful laugh. "Not the way I planned, though, now is it?" He set his luggage down and began to leaf through a stack of mail as though he were indifferent to her presence. "You're here because of Amber, aren't you?" he said quietly.

"You said then that it didn't matter that I was married to Hamlin, that you couldn't get me out of your mind."

"I was a little drunk that day, wasn't I? And I apologized later."

"Yes."

"And what did you say that next afternoon—and so sweetly, dear Serena—when I came by and said how sorry I was for behaving like such an idiot?"

"I don't remember."

"Well, I do. 'Be happy, Jake. Why don't you find some other woman to amuse yourself with?'"

"You should be pleased, Serena. I followed your advice." His low voice was filled with mockery.

"I'm the furthest thing from pleased," she retorted coldly.

"So I see," he murmured. "But then, you always were a difficult woman to make happy."

"I've come here to beg you to quit seeing Amber. You're just using her to make me jealous."

His cool eyes swept her. "What makes you say that?"

"Because I know you."

For the first time, he let his eyes meet hers. "And are you jealous?"

"That's not the point. Use someone else! She's Hamlin's sister, for heaven's sake! She's a wonderful girl, and she's had a bad time. I won't have her pulled between the two of us while we sort out the mess we've made of our lives. She deserves some fine man who can love her for herself.

"At least we're in agreement there."

"You're twisting my words."

"Have you come to offer yourself in her place?"

Her eyes held a hint of wildness, of the desire to rush away.

"I—I'm married to Hamlin."

"And you always will be. I've accepted that. And I'm a single man in need of feminine companionship. I happen to find Amber...er...amusing. I believe that was your word, my dear."

"Oh! You'll never change!" Serena sprang from the recliner and rushed toward him. Because he was afraid of those red-tipped claws and the wildness in her eyes, he pulled her into his arms. Then his hands closed over her wrists.

"Don't you think you're being selfish, Serena?" he whispered softly. "You have Hamlin, and I have no one. Do you really expect me to remain a bachelor for the rest of my life?"

She stared up at him, her eyes filling with horror. "Surely you wouldn't go so far as marriage?"

He met Serena's wide eyes, but it was Amber he saw. Amber with her slanting blue eyes and fiery hair. Amber, whose body was long-limbed and lush. Amber, watching him swim naked. Amber, hanging on the side of the cliff. Amber, on fire with desire as she melted in his arms. Amber, open and vulnerable.

For a long moment he was too stunned to say anything as he realized that, when he thought of Amber, the idea of marriage was not as repugnant to him as it always had been in the past.

Serena pulled herself free with a look of disgust. "I never thought you'd stoop this low to get even."

"Did it ever occur to you that maybe I don't want to get even? That maybe I just want Amber?"

"I'll never believe that!"

He reached out and cupped her chin gently with his hand. "Believe it. And, Serena, don't be so upset. We can't have each other. I've accepted that. Why shouldn't I marry someone else? Why not Amber?"

"Stop seeing her, Jake. I can't bear the thought of having you for my brother-in-law. I promise this is the last thing I'll ever ask of you. You'll only hurt her. If you ever cared anything for me, promise me this one thing."

For a long moment he was silent. Then he said very softly, "That's something I can't promise, Serena, not even to you."

"Jake, she's not playing games. She's in love with you."

His brown face was still. "How do you know?"

"She told me. If you can't return her love, whatever you think you can give her will never be enough."

Serena turned and ran then. He started to follow, then turned and walked slowly back inside the house.

It was late when Jake picked up the phone and dialed Amber. He'd been sitting in the darkness for hours. Thinking about Amber. About what Serena had said.

About his problems with the resort. Hell, if he wasn't careful, he might lose everything.

Serena was right. Amber deserved so much more than he could give her.

When Amber answered, he hesitated, then plunged into the conversation.

"This is Jake."

"I'm glad you're back."

She sounded breathless, wonderful. He was dying to see her. To hold her.

He imagined her lying in her bed, looking soft and sweet in a low-cut nightgown, her red hair fanning over the pillows. At the mere thought, he broke into a cold sweat. His body was stiff and hard with longing. What was he, crazy?

"I got in this afternoon," he said, already hating himself for what he was going to do.

"Oh." The one word held electric pain.

"I know I said something last week about us having dinner together tonight..."

"It doesn't matter."

He could tell that it did. Very much.

He went on. "But I was tired. I had a tough time in Denver."

"I'm sorry, Jake. I was hoping things would work out for you."

"Yeah. Me too." There was an awkward silence. White knuckles clenched the phone in a death grip. "Look, I'm tired. I've got a lot on my mind. And I'm going to be pretty busy the next few months. Maybe we'll run into each other some time."

The comfortable brush-off line. Only this time it didn't feel comfortable. It clogged his throat and made him feel slightly sick to his stomach.

"Maybe..." Her voice was faint. Hurt.

It cut him to the quick.

He drew a shaky hand across his face, brushing black hair from his damp brow. He had no choice. He was damn near broke. Amber deserved more than he could offer her. He wasn't sure he was in love, and if he wasn't in love with her, what were his real feelings? He cared about her too much to date her as casually as he dated other women.

"Jake, Serena was at your ranch this afternoon, wasn't she? Is that why..." She couldn't go on.

His heart had begun to thud violently. "As a matter of fact she did drop by," he admitted carefully. "How did you know that?"

"I was out riding Golden, and I saw her car on the road," Amber managed in a small, toneless voice. "Oh, Jake, how could you? Doesn't it bother you that she has a husband and son?"

He was stunned that she considered him capable of something so low. "Look, Amber," he began, his voice harsh in his pain.

She cut him off. "You don't have to explain anything to me, Jake Kassidy. I understand."

"No, you don't."

She didn't hear him. She had already hung up.

"Damn!" he muttered in the silence.

He felt alone. And miserable. And suddenly terribly restless.

He picked up the little black book beside the telephone, in which were written the numbers of all the women he knew. He thumbed the pages. Then he opened a drawer and tossed the book inside.

He swore softly, bitterly, under his breath.

There was only one woman he wanted, and he'd decided that he couldn't have her.

With an inarticulate cry of rage, he banged his fist on the table.

He had to have her.

But he wouldn't let himself.

Chapter Twelve

All hearts break differently. Some desperately. Some quietly. Some madly.

Amber's followed the latter course.

She was wrapped in pain, clawed by the inner agony of a deep, concealed wound.

Sometimes she felt smothered and afraid, like a child alone and lost in the dark, a child who remembers the warm glow of love and is baffled because it is lost to her. She wanted to cry out, but she knew there would be no one to answer her, and she was so fiercely proud, she was determined that no one sense her suffering. Most of all not Serena or Jake.

So it was a brave face Amber put on for the world. She let Hamlin get her blind dates, and she began to go out in the evenings. She started seeing Jim again.

She danced. And she sang. And she pretended.

When she felt like crying she laughed instead, and hoped no one noticed how hollow it sounded.

Her life became a whirlwind, and she pushed herself until she wanted to drop. Perpetual blue shadows appeared beneath her eyes; she grew thinner. Nothing mattered to her except running, except hiding from the pain locked deep inside her.

Though she tried not to think of Jake, she thought of him constantly. She knew that he was dating other women again, and she had to fight to pretend she didn't care when Hamlin or Serena mentioned casually that they had seen him somewhere with someone beautiful.

Amber threw herself into her work with the same desperate determination she did everything else, disappearing into her shop before Serena and Hamlin came down for breakfast, and not leaving until after they'd had supper. Then she would go upstairs, dress and go out.

Just when she most needed the money from her jewelry sales, her jewelry stopped selling. Sheila said not to worry, that jewelry sales always fell between the summer season and the ski season. But because she had been counting on the money so desperately, Amber could not help worrying.

After the threatening telephone call that night in Serena's presence, Amber had withdrawn the money she had kept in her bank account to pay her federal income taxes and mailed it to Don. For a time there were no more calls.

One afternoon, when Serena and Hamlin had taken Dave into Denver to see a rodeo and spend the night, Amber stopped working earlier than usual. She decided to ride Golden out across the desert toward the mountains. She wanted to be alone to face the pain she'd been so desperately trying to escape.

Though it was late October, it was an unusually balmy day, almost a summer day thrown down in the midst of autumn, and all the more precious for it. Amber held the reins loosely, letting Golden follow her own path across the desert, and eventually horse and woman came to the stream fed by a warm spring, where she'd seen Jake swim naked that long-ago summer day.

Amber dismounted, walked to the water's edge, and dipped her fingers into the sparkling stream.

It seemed even warmer than before, perhaps because the day was cooler.

Sunlight made dancing ribbons of light on the glassy surface. In her mind's eye she saw Jake as he'd been that day. A giant of a man, his body thick with bronzed muscle, and so sexy even his naked feet had seemed beautiful. She had wanted him even then.

The warm, glimmering water seemed to invite her.

She was all alone, wasn't she? She scanned the desert. There wasn't even a bird flicking across the immense blue sky and the pink horizons.

Slowly she unknotted her scarf, and let the soft yellow silk slide across her skin, over the tip of her flannel-covered bosom. She watched the bright yellow rectangle flutter down to the red sand where it lay curling in the faint breeze. Then she began to unbutton her blouse. When she hesitated, the wind ruffled its soft edges against her breasts.

She had never swum naked. All her life she had been too inhibited.

Something reckless came over her.

She pulled her blouse off, then her bra. The wind felt cool against her nipples. She stripped off her boots and her jeans.

Her heart was filled with a mad, all-consuming anguish. She didn't care anymore. It didn't matter what she said, how she lived.

She had always wanted love, and it had always eluded her.

She took a deep breath and dove into the warm bubbling water. She splashed across the pool, swimming back and forth, reveling in the new sensation of water sliding against her bare skin, almost exulting in this freedom she'd never known before.

To hell with Jake Kassidy. She was going to live as she'd never lived in the past. But as she thought of him, loneliness washed over her, and in the sparkling sunshine the loneliness seemed more poignant than ever before. She kicked the water with a vengeance. She wished she'd never known him. Never fallen in love with him. For the thousandth time she wondered where she would find the strength to go on.

Amber. Jake lay against the red cliff, letting the rough rocks cut into his back, almost welcoming the pain. He couldn't stop thinking about her. She haunted him.

Every minute of every hour of every day.

Damn!

His eyes were closed, but he saw her as if she stood before him in the blazing sunlight, her fiery hair billowing in the wind, her beautiful pale face, her intense blue eyes. He remembered how much bluer they became when they grew hot with desire.

He thought of all the things he wanted her to do to him. How he wanted her naked under his body, her hand running over his legs, lightly caressing, teasing. How he wanted to touch her himself until she was weak and quivering beneath his hand. Then he would kiss her. He knew from experience just how sweet she was to kiss. He remembered her taste. Her scent. The velvet-soft warmth of her skin.

It was what he didn't know from experience that was driving him crazy.

Damn it. He should have slept with her. Then maybe it wouldn't be so hard to forget her. She couldn't possibly be as good as he imagined her.

He opened his eyes to banish the tantalizing ghost.

And there she was, down below, in his stream. Only, she was real. An earthy goddess, and she was as naked as the day she was born.

Jake's heart began to pound violently, and he froze in a low crouch at the top of the ridge, his body white-hot with need. She looked so deliciously languid, it was obvious it had never occurred to her that this was a favorite spot of his, that it hadn't been a freak happening, his coming here to swim that first day when he'd caught her watching him.

She was floating on top of the water, her hair drifting away from her face in fan-like streamers of fire, her white, slender body open to his gaze. His eyes caressed the curves of her breasts, the slimness of her waist, her long, perfectly formed legs.

Desire flooded through him, a sharp hot pain, hardening his body. Suddenly he couldn't remember all the noble reasons he had for avoiding her. Even if he could, they didn't matter anymore.

The savage pulsing of his blood told him he wanted her, and that he wanted her as he'd never wanted any other. He had to feel her velvet skin beneath his hands and lips. He wanted to kiss her. To taste her.

Everywhere.

Would she be virginal or wanton?

He had to know.

Slowly he began to climb down the ridge.

Small rocks skidded under his black sharkskin boots, but she didn't hear him even though he didn't try to be quiet.

She was swimming across the stream in a great burst of speed when he reached the bank.

"How's the water?" The rough voice didn't sound like his own at all.

She gave a sharp little scream, and her body twisted in a shower of white spray.

"J—Jake," she quavered. Startled blue eyes met the intense blaze of his own. Her face flamed stop-sign red before she dove quickly under the water.

He was ripping off his shirt when she surfaced.

Her eyes flew to meet his once again. "What do you think you're doing?" she cried, lowering her gaze to his wide brown shoulders.

He grinned boldly at her. "You should know. You watched me before. Or don't you have your contacts in?"

Oh, she had them in. She was using them to study those well-muscled arms, the thick curls of black hair in the center of his broad chest and the way the black pelt tapered down the middle of his belly.

Her breath stopped, something fluttering in the pit of her stomach at his uncompromising masculinity. She watched in horror as he yanked his belt carelessly through denim belt loops and let it snake to the ground on top of her bright yellow scarf.

Oh, why did the mere sight of rippling muscle make her feel weightless in the water? As if she were melting into the warm liquid? Her breath stopped again.

He was fumbling with the button at his waistband. His legs were thrust wide apart in the age-old male stance.

There was a wildness inside her. A feeling of urgent expectancy that made her stiffen warily.

And she wanted to hate him!

A little whimper escaped her parted lips.

She jerked her eyes back up to his face. Who did he think he was? The arrogant strutting devil! He'd deserted her as if she were nothing. Left her while he enjoyed other women. Broken her heart.

She tilted her head back proudly, defiantly. She would die before she let him touch her.

"You'd better not come near me, Jake Kassidy." Her teeth were beginning to chatter, and not from the cold.

His wide grin could have belonged to a conquering warlord intent on ravishing a maiden he held prisoner.

"It's my land, and I guess that makes this my river. You're the one who's trespassing, Amber."

His jeans parted.

"Th-then if you'll just turn away, I'll gladly leave."

"But I won't just turn away." Again he grinned boldly. He'd like to meet the man who could. "I see it as my civic duty to punish all trespassers," he whispered. "Or reward them, as the case may be. Personally." The last word died away.

As he pulled his jeans off she dove under the water again. When she started to surface, Jake was in the water beside her. He grabbed her by the arm and dragged her hard against the scorching heat of his body.

She kept trying to move backward, into deeper water, out of his reach, but he kept up with her easily.

She didn't know what to do. Every time she struggled, her body touched his more intimately, and every time his skin passed fleetingly against hers, there came a peculiarly sensual feeling of skin warmed by hot skin, of tingling hot bubbles flowing up between them.

In the clear water there was no way he could conceal the blatant state of his arousal. Not that he seemed ashamed of it.

He put his arms around her waist and pressed full-length against her.

Bristly body hair brushed satin-smooth skin. And other things brushed together.

A queer thrill rippled through her.

"You, bastard..." she murmured.

"Call me anything you like," he murmured back in a subdued, humble tone. "I have it coming."

Suddenly she was weeping.

"I didn't want to hurt you," he said softly.

He took her hand in his and brought it to his lips, kissing the fevered pulse in the slender white wrist ever so gently.

Her hand was so small and smooth against his thicker, muscled one, so vulnerable and appealing. Or was it just that he was so desperately in need, every part of her seemed sexy to him?

"Forgive me, Amber."

"You have no right to do this," she pleaded.

He turned her hand over in his and lightly kissed the center of her palm, each fingertip.

"No right at all," came her voice, tinier than before. Her tears had stopped.

"This is my river. My land," he whispered.

"But..."

He put his arms around her and kissed her, a long kiss that went on breath after breath.

"And you're my woman."

His lips covered hers again. Moister than the stream. Hotter than the bubbling water. And no matter how hard he kissed her, it wasn't hard enough for either of them.

"Am I your woman, Jake?" she managed. Her eyes were as blue and luminous as the glistening stream. "What about all the others?"

"There aren't any others, you little fool."

"You keep dating."

"So do you."

"That was only because I'd go crazy thinking about you if I didn't."

"I know."

"What about Serena?"

Amber felt his muscles tighten.

"She's married," he said fiercely.

"I didn't think you cared about that."

"But I do. Forget Serena. If she mattered to me, do you think I'd be like this with you now?"

"I don't understand."

"Maybe this will help." He pressed her body into his again, and took her breath away with his burning lips. Slowly they sank under the water, kissing each other until they had to have air more than each other, until Amber broke free and fought her way to the surface. He met her there and pulled her into shallow water.

With her glistening breasts half out of the water, she stood staring at him with a soft look of desire, her pale face glowing in the gentle sunlight. He watched the quiet rise and fall of her breasts as she breathed. The water seemed a sparkling veil covering the rest of her body.

He caught her to him, his warm breath touching her cheek, sending shocks down her spine. Every quivering sensation in her body yearned for him. She began to tremble.

"Maybe you only want me because you found me swimming naked in your pool."

"Maybe..." The one word was deep, throaty.

Once again he pulled her into his arms, and he felt her shaking.

"You're cold," he said gently, crushing her naked breasts against his chest to warm her with the heat of his body.

No, she wasn't cold. She felt steamy, hotter than she'd ever been before.

His hands ran over her body, touching her expertly in soft warm places, inflaming her.

She gasped a deep, tortured breath of delight.

"Touch me, too," he commanded hoarsely.

When her fingers circled him, he sucked in his breath. She could feel the tremor that coursed through the muscles of his body. His fingers clenched on her waist so hard they hurt her.

He lowered his mouth and took starved possession of hers. He was trembling against her, his arms shaking as they held her to him, his mouth shaking too as it plundered the voluptuous fullness of her lips.

He eased into her slowly, prolonging his pleasure and hers, the heat of her shooting through his veins like an explosion of molten fire.

At last she was his. There was a tenderness in him, a frightening softness toward her. He kissed her more gently than ever he'd kissed a woman, murmuring something low and inaudible against her mouth.

Amber moved away from him ever so slightly, and his hands pulled her back, holding her desperately close.

"Jake, I love you," she murmured. "I don't want to. But I do. And I'm afraid."

"Hush."

He moved into her again, and she sheathed him, warmly, wetly, her body caressing the length of him until every male nerve seemed to pulsate in the hot, secret center of his being. His muscles knotted.

He couldn't wait. But he had to. For her.

She clung to him shamelessly, trembling as violently as he.

And then he could wait no longer.

But it didn't matter, because her body was attuned to his in some miraculous way, and she instinctively reached the zenith of passion the moment he did.

Her blood surged, her heartbeat sounding in her ears as she moaned shudderingly, surrendering to the screaming thrill of a rapture as vivid and blazing-hot as the sun in the great empty blueness above them.

Her fingers dug into his shoulders as he pressed into her body.

She was cold. And hot. Liquid. And fire.

The current swept around them, but he held on to her, staying inside her. She felt limp, as if her whole body had turned to water.

Their bodies stayed tightly locked. He bent his brow to hers and rested his black head against hers, struggling to gain control of his ragged breathing.

She sighed, feeling wonderful, complete, a part of him, and apparently he felt wonderful, too, because he threw back his head and laughed softly. Then he stopped, his eyes seeking her face. He studied it for a long quiet moment, as though he found her beauty dazzling.

She heard her own laughter, huskier, different somehow. She felt as if it had been the first time for her, as if only now that she belonged to him had she become a woman.

Later he took her back to his house, where they made love again in his bed. The second time he made it last for hours.

Afterward she lay cradled in his arms, their moist bodies a relaxed tangle of limbs and sheets and long red hair. He let his hand wander over her, tracing her curves with his fingers, as if to make sure she was really his.

When the sun sank below the purple mountains, they were already asleep.

Moonlight streamed through the window onto Amber's still face. She twisted, but the light followed her everywhere.

She blinked her eyes against the white sparkle, slowly drifting awake.

She grew aware of an unpleasant feeling. Her left leg had a cramp in it, but when she tried to move she discovered it was caught in a vise.

Opening her eyes, she saw Jake's black head nestled beside hers in the shower of silvery light. The vise holding her leg was his body.

She pushed at him, gently but insistently.

His black lashes feathered open, and he gazed into her eyes.

When she pushed at him again, he rolled off her.

There was a moment's silence between them.

"Are you sorry?" she whispered.

"Sorry?" One black brow arched quizzically.

"About us?"

He felt his body stir and come to life against her warm thigh. "Why would I be sorry?" he replied lazily.

"You never called," she whispered, a note of anguish in her voice. "All those weeks, you never called."

He drew her closer, into the circle of his arms, very gently. "But I wanted to."

"How do I know that?"

"Because I'm telling you." His eyes caressed her face.

"What about all those other women?"

"I told you."

"Tell me again."

"I was trying to forget you. Besides, you weren't exactly home cooling your heels."

"Jake, I missed you."

"I missed you too."

And somehow she knew he had. "Did anyone ever tell you your eyes are the color of jade?" she said.

"I don't believe they did."

"Jake with the jade-green eyes. Make love to me again, Jake."

He buried his lips in her throat, her hair, and felt her warmth against him. Her scent flowed into his nostrils. "I don't know if I can."

She bent her head and kissed him lightly, her tongue teasing his lips. His fingers cupped her breasts.

He held himself still, letting her fragrant warmth and sweetness slowly envelop him. She stirred against him.

Amber listened to his faint groan of pleasure with satisfaction.

When he made love to her, it was even more wonderful and piercingly fresh than before.

Afterward he wouldn't let her fall asleep again. She smiled, the gentle smile of satisfaction, and reached up to wind a thread of black hair between her fingers. In the moonlight, he gazed down upon her lovely face and into her drowsy, love-sated eyes. To imagine another man holding her in his arms evoked in Jake an unfamiliar, hellish jealousy.

His arms tightened around her, and he lowered his head and kissed her lips, lips that were still fever-warm from his lovemaking.

"I want to marry you," he said.

Softly shining blue eyes met the tenderness of his gaze.

"Why?"

"Because—" Hell, he could think of more reasons why they shouldn't than why they should. He ran a light finger over her belly. "I don't know why, Amber, I only know that I want you all to myself."

Her heart ached for words of love.

More softly, he said, "Amber, I need you. Marry me."

Chapter Thirteen

Marry Jake?

How could she? There was Don, and the fortune she owed the men in the Bahamas.

How could she not? She was in love, as she'd never been in love before.

Not that Jake had even considered taking no for an answer. When Amber had hesitated, he'd refused to let her go home, forcing her to spend the night gathered closely in his arms. She'd awakened to his lips moving slowly along her body. Then she'd felt his heaviness on top of her, the blazing warmth of him inside her, and he'd made love to her all over again.

Afterward Jake had held her against himself, his body still burning hot, and demanded that she marry him, and she'd found herself laughing shyly and consenting. Only then had he allowed her to ride Golden

home, and she'd made it back to the ranch just before
Serena and Hamlin returned with Dave from Denver.

Amber was in her shop, staring out the window toward the pink fringe of mountains that marked the
western boundary of the Kassidy Ranch, when she
heard an excited scuffle at her door.

"Aunt Amber! We're home!"

Amber ran her fingers through her disheveled hair in
a vain attempt to straighten it, while metal clanked
against the wooden door.

Dave burst through the door and threw his toy fire
truck onto the floor.

"Amber, darling." Serena smiled at her from across
the room.

Hamlin stepped inside. "Hope you didn't get too
lonely while we were gone."

Amber blushed hotly, her eyes falling away from
theirs.

"Any calls?"

"No."

Hamlin laughed. "Don't tell me nothing momen-
tous happened while we were out of town. Usually this
place is a tomb only until I leave."

"Nothing happened," Amber said.

Nothing much. She'd only taken a lover and then
promised to marry him.

Hamlin kept studying her face as though he sensed
Amber was withholding something. There was a moment of awkward silence between the adults that went
unnoticed by the exuberant fireball who was dashing
across the room toward Amber's worktable.

Dave picked up a pencil-shaped pendant Amber had
been working on the morning before and studied it in
fascination.

"Hey, Aunt Amber," he cried, dropping the pendant and lifting a fragile bracelet, waving it around like a banner, "you sure didn't do much while we were gone."

Amber flushed, but Serena and Hamlin were so busy concentrating on their young son's wildness around Amber's fragile creations that they paid no attention to what he was saying.

Amber hurried forward and gently pried the delicate piece of jewelry from his fingers.

"Son," Hamlin began sternly, "you know what I told you about not touching Aunt Amber's jewelry."

"Aunt Amber always lets me."

Amber sat down and pulled the little boy onto her lap. "Careful, Davie. Hold it like this. You don't want to bend it, do you?" She handed the bracelet back to him, rumpling his bright red hair fondly. "Now, why don't you tell me about the rodeo?"

"You're going to have to come inside with me if I do, 'cause it's going to take me forever."

As Amber followed them into the house, the child described every event in colorful but scrambled detail.

"What did you like best about the rodeo, Davie?" Amber asked when he'd finished.

"The chocolate ice cream cone."

Hamlin groaned. "You could have stayed home and had that."

Serena, who was holding her husband's hand, laughed.

For the first time, Amber noticed how radiant Serena seemed that afternoon. She was softer somehow, more beautiful than ever, and she was less nervous and more attentive to Hamlin. When she wasn't actually touching him, her eyes followed him about the room..

When she ran out of cigarettes, she didn't rush upstairs for a fresh pack.

"Hamlin wants me to stop smoking," Serena said at one point, "and I think I'll give it a try."

"We didn't just go to the rodeo," Hamlin began, a twinkle in his eye.

"Don't, Hamlin," Serena begged.

"Why not? I'm proud of you."

"But I haven't done anything yet."

"You got a job with the most prestigious public-relations firm in Denver."

"What?" Amber was suddenly bubbling with curiosity.

What it means, sister dear, is that Serena won't be working free for you any longer."

"Of course I will," Serena said.

"While we were in Denver, I made an appointment for Serena at this public-relations firm. Let me tell you, I had to practically drag her there for an interview, but what do you know? They hired her on the spot. She's going to be a consultant, and she already has a shy young writer she's supposed to help promote."

"Why, that's wonderful, Serena," Amber exclaimed, amazed.

"Until you came to stay with us, Amber," Hamlin continued, "I never realized how important it is for a woman to have something of her own to do. I always thought marriage and a child should be enough. It never occurred to me that since I had the ranch and my business interests, Serena might start feeling at loose ends all by herself out here."

"It wasn't all that bad, Hamlin darling," Serena murmured, but her face was aglow.

"When Serena had such fun promoting you," Hamlin went on, "it started me thinking that she needed something I couldn't give her." He drew his wife into his arms and kissed her gently. "You're so independent, Amber, and we're both so proud of you."

Amber wrung her hands silently at what she felt was undeserved praise.

"You'll never know how much you've done for both of us by coming here, Amber," Hamlin continued. "I was taking Serena for granted, and we were beginning to drift apart."

Amber turned away from them, feeling uneasy. So Hamlin had not been as oblivious to Serena's unhappiness as she had believed. Oh, how she hoped he was right in thinking that a new interest was all Serena needed.

Amber remembered that afternoon several weeks earlier when she'd seen Serena roaring back from Jake's ranch. How guilty and upset Serena had been that night. She had even lied at dinner when Hamlin had asked her about her day.

Then Jake had called later that evening and broken his date with Amber. Was that because he believed he could have Serena?

Was it really an outside interest Serena needed? Or was it a man that she couldn't have? For that matter, did she think she had him now? Was Jake the real reason Serena seemed happier?

Had Jake thought better of an illicit affair with a married woman? Had he only asked Amber to marry him as a last desperate attempt to forget Serena?

A bleak and bitter pain stole across Amber's heart. No!

Amber was determined to give Jake the benefit of the doubt even though she felt as if she were dying inside.

Later that same day, Jake came by.

As soon as Amber saw his truck she flew down the stairs, across the wooden porch and into his arms.

Serena and Hamlin and Dave were coming around the house from the barn, and for a fleeting instant Amber saw their incredulous faces.

Amber closed her eyes, and the faces blurred to nothingness. Her heart was hammering wildly as Jake's lips took hers.

I don't care! I don't care what they think! she thought, a sweet madness sweeping over her as she stretched onto her tiptoes. She was going to marry Jake Kassidy, and that was all that mattered.

Little feet stamped impatiently on wooden stairs. "Hey, you don't look very mad at Uncle Jake to me, Aunt Amber," Dave cried as Jake gently released her.

Smiling, Jake knelt down beside the little boy. "I'm going to marry your aunt Amber, and after that I'll be your real uncle."

Behind them there was a startled cry and Amber looked over Jake's broad shoulder. Serena's hands were covering her lips. Her face was washed of color, and she seemed to sink into Hamlin.

"Hello, Serena," Jake murmured with gentle concern as he saw her for the first time. "Hamlin..." Jake nodded and then stood up slowly, extending his hand to Hamlin as Hamlin and Serena stepped onto the porch.

Hamlin stood there looking at Jake, then at Amber, whose face was radiant. Serena kept her eyes downcast.

Somehow they all got past that first silent moment of shock.

"I could do with a scotch," Jake said at last.

"Make that a double," said Serena throatily.

Hamlin was at the bar in the den mixing everyone a drink. The two women stood at opposite windows.

Jake was restlessly pacing the den in long fluid strides. "Hamlin, you can't mean Amber didn't even drop a hint about us!"

"I knew she was hiding something! What happened? When I left, you two hated each other."

"We accidentally bumped into one another while you were in Denver."

"It must have been one hell of a bump."

Amber blushed. Her eyes flew to Jake's twinkling ones, only to find that he was grinning boldly at her. She glanced quickly away, her blush deepening.

"Everything always happens when I'm gone!" Hamlin said unhappily.

"Then this is one time I'm glad you left, old friend," Jake murmured, savoring for a moment the pleasant memory of Amber in his pool. She was a wanton; wilder than even his wildest fantasies. His mind filled with the feel of her body, warm and soft against his. "If you hadn't, I might not be getting married next week.

"N-next week!" Serena choked. She was deathly pale, her mouth fixed in a frozen smile. "Surely that's rushing things a bit, even for you, Jake." Her white fingers picked up a pack of cigarettes and shook one out.

Jake reached in his pocket for his lighter. Amber watched them come close together as he lit her cigarette; their black heads almost touched, then drew apart.

Hamlin was watching them too.

"I think it's great!" Hamlin said emphatically, going to his wife's side and putting his hand lightly around the back of her waist as though to assert possession. "This means Amber will be staying on with us permanently."

"Not with us, Hamlin," Serena corrected. "She'll be married to Jake."

"That's all to the better."

Serena exhaled two jerky puffs of smoke.

"Amber wants to be married here, in your house, Serena, but if that's inconvenient—" Jake began quietly.

"It's not that it's inconvenient," Serena answered, "it's just—"

"Good," Jake said. "Then it's settled. Next Sunday."

"Next Sunday..." Serena's voice trailed away.

"Next Sunday! Whoopee!" Dave cried. "A wedding! Aunt Amber, can I be your flower boy?"

Never had a week passed faster. Jake was more interested in the honeymoon plans than he was in the actual ceremony, but he wouldn't tell Amber where they were going.

"Just describe the sort of place you'd like to go," he'd said.

She was thinking of Don and the man who wanted money from her. "I want to run away with you forever, somewhere where nobody can find us. An island with cliffs and crashing waves."

He'd laughed.

"Somewhere alone with you," she'd finished.

"That's exactly what I had in mind." His hot gaze drifted over her body. "But who says we have to wait until our honeymoon for that?"

Amber spent two days designing a wedding ring and making it for Jake, but when she showed it to him, she could tell he wasn't pleased.

He was statue-still, fingering the golden circlet, regarding it dubiously as he held it to the sunlight.

"Try it on," she urged, eagerness lighting her eyes.

He tried to look thrilled, but he handled the ring as if it were an alien object. "I don't usually wear jewelry," he said at last.

Her hand closed over the warmth of his. "But Jake, this is different." Her voice was soft. "This means that you belong only to me. Forever."

Her words seemed to make up his mind. Very carefully, he set the ring in the center of her open palm and folded her fingers over it one by one.

"You're not going to wear it ever, are you?" she cried.

"I didn't say that," he said quietly.

"Maybe you don't want to belong only to me."

He bent over her hand and brushed a kiss upon it. Jade-green eyes rose to hers. He paused, fumbling for the right words.

"I'm marrying you, Amber. I want to spend the rest of my life with you. Isn't that enough?"

He had never said he loved her. Never once. Yet there was something in his eyes that consumed her.

She gripped the ring so tightly the metal edges cut into her flesh. With great effort she managed a tremulous smile. "Sometimes I'm not sure, Jake."

"Then maybe it's time I convinced you all over again."

His large bronzed hands stole to her face and tilted it upward. Gently he kissed her.

Gradually, beneath the warm onslaught of his mouth, her tension eased. His kiss deepened, and she felt as hot as a melting candle. The old trembling possessed her. Her hand relaxed, and the ring fell through her fingers and rolled across the table, falling to the floor with a clink.

Neither of them heard the tiny sound. They were too enthralled with the rapture they found in each other. It was only later, after he had gone, that Amber found it lying forgotten in a dark corner. It was only then, as she picked it up, that all her old doubts came back to haunt her.

Jake didn't love her, and he didn't intend to lie to her.

It was the day of the wedding. The inside of the house was festooned with flowers; outside a blizzard raged, despite the fact that a week before they had swam on an Indian summer's day. Because of the blizzard, there were few witnesses to observe their exchange of vows as Amber and Jake stood beside one another before the preacher. One was Paula, her white brows knotted with concern. Beside her stood a pale Serena and an exuberant Hamlin. Davie was there, of course, and the neighbors who lived nearest.

Still, to Amber it was like a dream, Jake's standing there dark and silent, so elegant and handsome in his black suit. It seemed to Amber that Jake was the one dream in her life that had really come true.

She held her breath as onto her finger he slid a beautiful wedding ring, set with amber and jade twined in gold, that he had had made for her. Later, when he lifted her veil and bent down to kiss her, she felt breathless again.

His arms slid around her waist and he crushed her to him, then pressed his mouth down on hers just as tightly in a kiss that went on and on.

Jake had forgotten the occasion.

Hamlin coughed. Everyone laughed, and Jake let her go.

In a daze of happiness, Amber went through the rituals of matrimony. Afterward it would all seem a dream: Hamlin flushed with pride and good humor, drinking too much champagne at the reception, making too many toasts; Davie stuffing himself with wedding cake, his eyes round with awe every time he looked at the bride and groom; and Serena, white-faced and lost, hovering apart from the others, silently watching Jake.

Finally the long day was nearing an end, and Amber left Jake alone in the den while she went upstairs to change. Jake settled into an easy chair and watched the snow fall and whirl away in the wind. He was glad his truck had four-wheel drive, and that he'd taken the trouble to put chains on his tires. The last thing he wanted was a breakdown on the road.

All day Amber's innocence in her wedding gown had tantalized him. He kept remembering her naked in his pool, her body flaming hot against his, her eyes enticing. At the memory of her eager passion his body tightened.

Now she was his wife. Mrs. Jake Kassidy.

He heard a soft sound at the door and he got up, thinking it was Amber. Instead, Serena stepped inside and raised one finger to her lips to indicate silence as she shut the door behind her.

"J-Jake—" Her voice was hoarse, and for a moment she couldn't go on.

Jake looked down at the floor, avoiding her eyes.

"J-Jake, I know it's not the custom, but will it be all right if I kiss the groom?"

"Oh, Serena..." He raised his head and looked at her.

She was as beautiful as ever with her black hair and dark eyes, and he was too stunned by her sudden appearance and her air of mystery to notice that the violent tug of desire she'd always aroused in him wasn't there twisting his heart.

Serena stared at him, her eyes wide, her lips softly parted.

Slowly he went to her and circled her with his arms.

"Our last kiss," she murmured.

As his lips touched hers, there was a muffled noise at the door, but neither of them heard it.

Amber pushed open the door and saw them through the tiny crack. She wanted to sink through the floor and vanish forever, but she stood there, rooted by her despair. Her heart felt stabbed by a knife of ice, and the coldness grew, deepening inside her until it consumed every part of her.

She bit into her lower lip, and only the bitterness of her own blood stopped her from crying out.

Why? Oh, why?

She couldn't fathom such cruelty. How could he! And on their wedding day!

Somehow she pulled her fingers from the cold brass doorknob and stumbled backward toward the stairs that led to her bedroom.

Inside the den, Serena had begun to cry. "I'll never get over you, Jake, just as you'll never get over me."

Gently Jake disentangled himself. "Don't, Serena. This is my wedding day."

Her next sob broke louder than before.

"Serena, you were the one who wanted me to have a life of my own."

"I didn't know then how unbearable it would be."

"I'm going to be a good husband to Amber, Serena."

"But you don't love her."

"There are different kinds of love. You love Hamlin, don't you?"

"Don't you see? That's how I know the hell you're in for. Yes, I love him, but he doesn't make me feel the way you did."

"We were just kids."

"All you'll ever have with Amber is a pale imitation of what we had."

"Maybe I don't want what we had anymore, Serena. It sure as hell didn't work out, for either of us. We were both too strong, always pulling at each other. Always going in opposite directions. Maybe, it's time we faced this thing, and put it behind us for good."

"If only we could."

"I wouldn't be marrying Amber if I didn't think it would work, Serena. Hell, most people probably have old loves tucked away somewhere like skeletons in dark closets."

"I wish that was where you were, Jake Kassidy! I was happier before you came back! If only you'd go away, I wouldn't be constantly reminded that I gave you up. Instead you're my next-door neighbor, and now my brother-in-law!" With a little cry, Serena whirled blindly toward the door.

Jake made no attempt to stop her.

* * *

Slowly Amber sank down upon Jake's bed, wondering desperately what she should do. How could she and Jake go on together as man and wife after what she'd witnessed that afternoon? She set the blouse she'd been unpacking on top of the bed and stared listlessly out the window.

Jake and Serena. Her poor brother and herself caught in the middle. Even though Amber had suspected, she hadn't quite let herself believe, and she was devastated. And yet...

Was it really so impossible to go on? Would Jake have married her if he didn't intend to try to forget Serena?

After she'd discovered Jake and Serena together, the rest of the afternoon had been unendurable. Somehow, Amber had managed to keep smiling, to keep pretending. People had patted her hand, congratulated her. She'd thrown the bouquet from the landing, driven back to Jake's ranch wrapped in his arms, and now it all seemed only a dimly-remembered blur of pain.

Suddenly she heard Jake on the stairs, and her heart began knocking all over again.

He opened the door. Her every instinct screamed for her to run, but there was no place she could go.

She was his wife. This was their wedding night. Outside, a winter storm raged.

Oh, dear God.

"I thought you came upstairs to undress," he said huskily.

"I—I..."

Their eyes met, then she jerked hers quickly away. He moved into the room and crossed the floor. She watched silently as he unbuttoned his shirt and stripped it off.

The soft lamplight bathed him with its golden glow, and something caught in her throat at the sight of him. Even when she was reeling from hurt, she thought him magnificent. There was such power in his broad tanned shoulders and muscular arms, such virile masculinity in the thick mat of hair covering his wide chest and hard flat stomach. She was aware of a quiver in the pit of her stomach.

Oh, why couldn't he love her?

"You're awfully quiet tonight, Amber," he said, tossing his white shirt over the back of a nearby chair and coming toward her.

He was lithe teak muscle. Hard flesh. Man.

She stiffened as he knelt beside her and drew her into his arms. "J-Jake, please let me go." Her voice was breathless, hoarse with the threat of tears.

"You're my wife," he muttered thickly. "I've been waiting all day for this moment." He stared down at her, and she shut her eyes helplessly as his mouth came down upon hers.

His lips were hard and hot, taking what they wanted from her trembling mouth. His hands were everywhere, exploring every curve. She fought not to react, but despite her hurt, his fingers running intimately over the tips of her breasts caused a tingle in her belly. It would be so easy to surrender to Jake's magnetism, to relax and let her senses take over. So easy to pretend that what she'd seen had never happened. But she was determined never again to run away from reality.

Amber forced her slim hands to reach up and push against the smooth brown warmth of his chest. Beneath his lips, her mouth was stiff and unresponsive. He let her go. She felt his eyes upon her, emerald-dark and questioning.

"What's wrong?" he murmured. "You've hardly said a word for hours."

"I don't feel like talking," she mumbled. She could still taste the flavor of his mouth, still feel the feverish warmth of his body, and the tantalizing desire he aroused in her almost made her forget her resolution.

"I don't feel like talking either." His low voice was suggestive, and his hand started to curl over hers before she snatched it away.

"Just, please, go away, Jake. I don't want you to touch me or make love to me."

"You can't mean that, darling. You're just tired."

He reached for her, but she shrank away. "No! I don't want you, or anything from you—ever again."

She got up, intending to escape him somehow, and then a hand gripped her arm, spinning her around so that she was looking into his eyes again. His handsome face was dark with fury.

"Why in the hell did you marry me, then?" he demanded.

"Shouldn't I be the one to ask that question, Jake?"

"What do you mean?"

He seemed genuinely puzzled, and that only made her angrier.

"Why do you even bother pretending it's me you want? I saw you with Serena in the den. Did you kiss her with your mouth half-open and tell her you were dying for her? How often have you made love to her in that same pool the way you made love to—"

He made no answer.

Wretched with anguish, Amber lunged toward him, raising her hand to slap him, but he caught her slim wrist and held it with crushing force.

"What else have you done together, Jake? Will I only be a poor substitute for the nights when you can't have her?" The tears had begun to race in earnest down her cheeks.

His face was very still. "It wasn't what you think, Amber."

"No? Then she's just one of many?"

"Damn you," he muttered, more furious than before.

"You've never once told me you love me, Jake," she whispered.

His intense eyes held hers; the moment of silence between them stretched endlessly.

Then she wrenched free and tried to run from him again. He pulled her back easily, spinning her around so that his face was only inches from hers.

"Why, Jake?"

"It's you I want, damn it."

"But you don't love me."

"Whatever I felt for Serena in the past, I would never have married you if I intended to be unfaithful to you," he said coldly. "Is that so hard to believe?"

"How can I believe you after what I saw?"

"Serena came to the den and said she wanted to kiss the groom. Every man at the wedding kissed you."

"Not like that. Oh, Jake, not even I am that gullible."

"There's something called trust."

"You ask too much, Jake."

"Then there's nothing I can say?"

"Nothing."

He seemed to hesitate, his face hard and remote. Then he dropped his hands from her arms. He got up and lit a cigarette.

He was at the door now, standing in the shadows. "You're such a child, Amber. You think because you want something, you should be able to have it instantly. Love isn't something you can demand like a new toy. It's something two people have to work for. I'm willing to do that."

"Jake, spare me the lies I want so terribly to believe."

"You don't have to worry, Amber," he said wearily. "Keep your precious body to yourself. Sleep alone tonight and every night for all I care. I can't force you to believe me, and I won't force myself on you. I'll just go."

She listened to his retreating footsteps. Down the hall, a door slammed.

Too miserable to sleep, Amber lay in the bed hour after hour watching the snow swirl against the windowpanes, her body aching to curl into the muscled length of Jake.

Jake. She kept remembering the haunted look on his face just before he walked out. Perhaps he had been telling the truth about Serena. And no matter what he felt for Serena, Amber decided, he must feel something powerful for her as well. Why else had he been so wild to marry her? He'd said he was willing to work on their marriage. What more could she ask of him?

It was past midnight when she flung the warm sheets aside and rose from her bed. In the freezing darkness, she began to shiver. Quickly she ran down the hall toward the guest bedroom, hesitating just outside the closed door, suddenly terrified of facing him.

It took all her courage to open the door and step inside.

She stood in the gloom, clutching her hands together to still their trembling.

Jake lay in bed, his black head propped against his crossed arms as he stared, brooding, at the ceiling.

Her voice was a whisper across the darkness. "Jake..."

"Amber?" From the bed came a slight rustling as he leaned forward.

"You weren't asleep?" she asked, feeling the terrible awkwardness between them.

"No."

"I couldn't sleep, either," she said nervously. "I wanted to talk to you."

"All right."

At the sight of her, the pulse in his throat had begun to beat savagely. She was standing without a robe in a pool of silvery light, and he could see the shape of her shivering body through her thin nightgown.

"Jake," she began breathlessly. "I came to say I'm sorry. I—I..." She paused, straining to see his expression, but she couldn't in the dark. "I shouldn't have been so quick to think you would treat me dishonorably. I don't know why—"

"You don't have to explain. I understand."

"You couldn't possibly," she whispered.

"Come here, darling."

"Not yet. There's something I have to say. Oh, Jake, don't you see? The reason I got so upset is because...you're all I have." Her voice broke. "A-all I've ever had."

There was a silence. After a long time he murmured, "Amber, you're all I have."

She stood there looking at him in that queerly-lighted darkness, his hair falling like a silver shower over his shadowed face, and it came to her anew that his life must have been every bit as lonely as hers. His father had died when he was still a boy. He had no brothers or sisters. The woman he'd grown up loving had married someone else. Now he lived out on his ranch in the middle of nowhere, all alone. Suddenly she wondered if, in his own way, he was running away from things just as she was. She'd been so busy focusing on her own problems she hadn't considered his. Who were Jake's allies? His friends? Everything he'd ever done, he'd done himself, alone. What kind of pain causes a man to isolate himself? She knew he hadn't wanted to become involved with her. That had been beyond his control. If she turned her back on him, who would he have?

Blindly she crossed the room. In one swift movement, he pulled her in bed beside him. Gently she placed her arms around him.

She was shaking, from the chill, from his nearness. He took both her cold hands in his and drew her beneath the covers against his body. Her nightgown slid up her legs, and she felt the smooth hardness of his bare skin, the rasp of coarse body hair against her own satin flesh. His hand wound into her hair, and he brought her face nearer to his.

In the dim light his skin was dark, his eyes a deep burning green. Her pulse began to throb so violently she could scarcely breathe as his mouth lowered to hers.

He kissed her until they were both breathless with hunger.

"I'm sorry too, Amber," he whispered against her parted lips. "I should have told you about Serena from the beginning, but I didn't want her coming between us. She's come between me and so much in my life. What I feel for you is something quite special. You must believe that.''

"I'll try, Jake. I promise you, I'll try."

His fingers fumbled with the silken fabric covering her breasts. He was unbuttoning her nightgown, sliding it downward until she lay beside him as naked as he.

A wave of inexplicable happiness swept away the pain of the long afternoon. She loved him, and if he didn't yet love her...

She realized she was determined to work for a happy marriage. Why should she ask more of him than she herself could give? She wasn't yet entirely convinced that in part she hadn't married him because he represented strength, because she was too dependent by nature to want to take care of herself.

If he was using her to conquer his past, wasn't she using him as well?

He gathered her into his arms, rolled beneath her, and pulled her on top of his body. They fitted together intimately, and a ripple of desire turned her blood to flame. Her fiery hair tumbled over her shoulders to his chest.

"I love you, Jake Kassidy." Her tone was awed, hushed, and he pulled her nearer to listen. "I can't help myself."

She sighed then laughed gently, as she thought that, even if he wasn't completely hers, he was her husband, her lover. Only hers. Tonight would be the first of the many times he would possess her as a husband possesses his wife. She longed for his warmth, his passion.

He dug his fingers into her hair and drew her face closer to his, but instead of taking her lips he nuzzled her throat, prolonging the aching suspense of their wanting.

She had longed for violent passion, not this tender gesture, but somehow his gentleness was infinitely more erotic. She felt his teeth against her flesh, their sharp edges ever-so-slightly caressing the throbbing heart-beat beneath delicate skin, and she shivered. He was holding himself in check, holding her in check. She was ravenous for him.

His calloused fingers stroked her body, touching her, then withdrawing his fingers, knowing instinctively how to make her catch her breath every time.

At her last indrawn gasp she felt him shaking.

Very slowly he drew her face into the light and stud-ied her. She closed her eyes, embarrassed by the avid intensity in his dark eyes.

"I didn't marry you to hurt you, Amber. I married you because I want to love you." His low tone was hoarse, and the faint tremor hinted at a powerful un-derlying emotion he was unable to express.

Then his mouth touched hers, and his gentle kiss sparked an explosion of white-hot, vivid sensations. Her arms wound around his neck, and her lips began to tremble over his.

The darkness closed over them, and he was dark-ness, and she was darkness, swirling away on a black rush of flame that consumed them.

Chapter Fourteen

Amber wished their honeymoon would go on forever, that somehow she could magically turn the three weeks of having Jake all to herself on the sun-drenched Spanish island of Ibiza into a lifetime of sparkling days followed by nights of passion.

But no matter how happy she was, every moment of joy was tinged with a silent desperation in her heart. Even when Jake made love to her and he seemed completely, irrevocably hers, after they drew apart, back into themselves, her silent doubts returned.

Because she was insecure, she found herself analyzing his every mood, and when he fell into brooding silences she grew wild with worry, wondering if he was beginning to regret their marriage. Then she would coax him from his mood, but long after his smiles returned, she never believed fully that he was hers.

Jake and Amber arrived on Ibiza, the smallest of the Balearic islands in the Mediterranean, two days after their wedding. It was midnight, and even though they were both exhausted from long flights and layovers, Jake rented a car. They laughed as it rattled and jounced over cobblestones and weather-worn roads, saying that the little vehicle seemed made of strung-together sardine cans.

She snuggled close to Jake, holding on to his hand, straining to see as they followed the twisting road into the dense midnight darkness that shrouded the island. The wind rose, and the night came alive with writhing trees.

Amber's window was open, and the air smelled of pine, salt, sea and the pungency of wild herbs. There was something oddly sensual about the darkness and the gusting fresh air, and Amber nestled closer to Jake. She could have driven forever, held close against him, letting the sweet-scented air play in her hair.

The road gave a triple twist, and Jake stamped down hard on the brake. They had arrived. Jake parked in front of an unpretentious lime-washed hotel nestled in a thicket of flowers, their blossoms loose and wind-blown.

The lobby was deserted. One dim lamp beside the guest register served as the only source of light. A buzzer was sounding at a switchboard, and an empty chair had been pushed aside.

Amber took Jake's hand and giggled nervously. "This place is so eerie I feel like we just stepped into one of those old horror movies, and all life on earth except us has been destroyed."

Jake chuckled and gathered her into his arms. "And we're the only man and the only woman left alive. That doesn't sound so bad."

"Like Adam and Eve," she whispered.

One of his fingertips grazed the line of her cheek. "That's a hell of a responsibility."

"What do you mean?"

His gaze was warm. "It's up to us to repopulate the world." There was a quiet intimate quality to this last low-toned statement.

She blushed, realizing that never before had he mentioned the possibility of their having a baby together. Even though she knew he was joking, it was a distinctly unsettling thought.

"Well, if we can just find our room, we can start repopulating," she said lightly, hoping her voice was as casual as his, so he wouldn't realize how deeply his off-hand remark had affected her.

"You said you wanted to go somewhere you could be alone with me." His green eyes were studying the lush curve of her mouth.

"Where no one could find us," she remembered.

"Well, here we are." His soft drawl was caressing. Everything he did, everything he said heightened the sensual undercurrents between them. "There aren't any phones in the rooms, and as you can see, the staff doesn't bother to answer the telephone, much less take messages."

"You're obviously a man who takes his woman at her word."

His eyes met hers. "Right now I'm a man who just wants to take his woman."

A little breathlessly she said, "Jake, you'd better ring for our room."

''To hell with our room. If we're the only man and the only woman . . .''

She started to protest, but it was too late. He was already tipping her head back to receive his kiss. Her hands wound around his neck, surrender quivering through her body down to her toes as his lips seared her. Strong hands forced her feminine shape to fit the hard contours of his male form. He arched her against his hip, the taut muscles of his leg sliding between hers.

The pressure of his mouth was demanding, seeking, ravishing. It was as though he were starved for her, and Amber didn't dare let the force of his passion build.

Her shaking fingers fumbled across the counter behind him, and finding the bell, she jammed her palm down on it.

At the bursts of sound, Jake dragged his mouth from hers. ''Traitor,'' he whispered.

A sleepy porter came out, signed them in and, promising to bring their bags, led them to their suite.

As they were leaving the lobby, the buzzer of the switchboard started again, but when Jake offered to wait, the porter shook his head and whispered, ''Mañana.''

''Mañana,'' Jake said in an undertone to Amber, ''our friend will doubtless say the same thing. No one can find us here, darling.''

She thought of the men in the Bahamas, and she wondered if he was right.

When the porter left them alone in their rooms, Jake began to unpack so he could take a shower first. Amber waited for him outside on the balcony.

The moon came out from behind a thick cloud-bank. A long splash of tarnished silver fell across the cliff beneath her, pouring down on to a beach hundreds of feet below, the light crinkling faintly on the tips of the waves and falling like dirty moon-powder onto the rocks and shivering trees.

The view was breathtaking, and it had an immediate and powerful effect upon Amber. It was so darkly awesome that she felt insignificant. Again she knew the sense of abandonment and miserable loneliness she'd known as a child, all those years ago when she'd so desperately wanted her mother's love.

Only now it was Jake's heart she sought so hopelessly. Jake's love.

It was her honeymoon, and she had Jake all to herself.

She should be happy.

Never had she felt more alone, nor more cut off from everyone else on earth.

Amber ran back inside the room, and Jake was there, naked, with the water from the shower glistening on his copper-hued muscles. There was tension in the broad sweep of his shoulders, smoldering passion in his green-dark eyes.

He was standing beside the bed. Without a word he stripped the bedcovers back.

In an instant her strange mood vanished. Wordlessly she crossed the room and melted into his arms. A long time later she said, "Why did you bring me here?" Her voice was softer than ever before.

"Because this is the most erotic place in the world."

"I'm not sure I can just take your word for that," she murmured.

"Then I'll have to prove it to you."

Twining his hands in her hair, he lowered his mouth to hers. His other hand began untying ribbons, loosening tiny buttons, unhooking snaps. Silk slid down velvet skin.

She was naked in the moonlight. Her ragged breath caught in her throat as he forced her body more intimately against his. She felt the mounting male power in him, throbbing and hard against her thigh.

He pulled her down to the bed and began to touch her and kiss her everywhere except those intimate secret places where she longed most to be touched. Deliberately, he made her wait. His tongue traced a lingering path from her breasts to her navel and then lower.

And at last, as he tasted her essence, Amber bit her lip on a long shudder that traveled the length of her naked body.

An animal moan rose in her throat. "Jake, please, let me make love to you."

He stopped kissing her.

She smiled, then bent over him and began to kiss him as he had kissed her. Passionate feminine lips explored and gently caressed, her moist tongue teasing and sweetly tormenting him, until he was as wild for her as she was for him.

He took her, seeking his release silently, swiftly, and it was more wonderful than it had ever been before.

Jake and Amber were inside a plush jewelry shop in the old city, Galeria Candone. Her shopping bag bulged with original jewelry made from precious and unusual metals. Jake had set his own stuffed bag, loaded with ceramics and two marble carvings, on the counter. He was fingering a gold necklace set with tiny diamonds.

"No, Jake, really! I couldn't possibly let you. It's far too expensive. Besides, you've already bought me too many presents."

"I didn't know a bridegroom could buy his bride too many presents on their honeymoon."

Amber looked at the lovely necklace glittering on Jake's dark wrist, and the most awful desire to have it rose within her. Then she frowned. Had she really changed? She was remembering how once she'd begged Don to buy her lavish gifts, how once she'd married him mainly because of what he could give her.

She tore her gaze from the sparkling thing. "I really don't need a necklace."

"Of course you don't need it. I want to buy it for you because it's beautiful and you're beautiful."

"No! Jake, I thought you had to be careful about money."

His brows came together, and she realized she had said the wrong thing.

"You are the most independent woman I've ever known."

If he only knew.

"I can afford to buy my wife a necklace. Hell, a few hundred dollars one way or the other won't matter."

She watched numbly as Jake pulled out his wallet. The saleswoman flashed her a triumphant smile.

"I said I didn't want you to buy it, Jake."

Jake handed the woman the money and completed the purchase. "But I've already bought it, darling." He picked up the necklace, and Amber allowed him to fasten it around her neck. "You're my wife," he said. "I want to buy you anything you like."

Amber started to say something, but she didn't want to quarrel. At last she said, "I shall be hopelessly spoiled."

It was later that same afternoon when she again brought up the subject of presents. They were wandering through the modern town of Santa Eulalia del Río, with its sheer cliffs and its tiers of lime-white condominiums built over the old town.

The salt breezes played in Amber's hair. She fingered the necklace he had bought earlier. "Jake, I want to love you for yourself, not for what you can buy me."

"I know. Your nonmaterialistic nature delights me, but it's going to take some getting used to. Just as my need to prove myself may take some getting used to on your part."

The air was hazy and golden, and with the ancient architecture it almost seemed they'd stepped into another century.

"The need to prove yourself?"

Jake stopped walking and pulled her against a ramshackle white wall.

"You see, Amber, I always thought Serena married Hamlin at least partially because he was rich and I wasn't. Maybe that's when I started equating money with success. Anyway, it became important to me to make money. I guess I decided I had to be the kind of man who could give a woman what she wanted. It's ironic. I married a woman who doesn't want any of the things I planned to give her."

"Would you prefer that I married you for your money?"

"No."

Amber couldn't be entirely certain of his answer. Did he want to buy her things because he couldn't give her what she really wanted, his heart?

Jake gave her no time for further thought. He folded her hand in his and grinned boldly. "There's a beach nearby. I read about it in the guidebook."

"I didn't bring my bathing suit."

His eyes twinkled. "Nobody wears bathing suits on this particular beach."

She blushed.

"Puritan," he teased, his devilish grin broadening.

"Do you mind?"

He shook his head. His mouth sought hers, and the instant their lips touched her heart began to race.

"It's not that I mind taking off my clothes," she said. "I'd just rather be alone with you when I do it."

"So would I."

His mouth lingered on hers, tantalizing her.

"You know you're right," she murmured, as the sensual excitement of his kiss spread through her. "There is something about this island."

"No, darling, it's you."

"And you," she whispered."

"Us."

They laughed huskily. Then his hands tightened around her shoulders, and as he deepened his kiss, the sultriness of the pine-scented island seemed to wrap them in the easy drift of its all-enveloping sensuality.

The moment Jake and Amber stepped off their plane in Denver, the honeymoon was over. They were no longer alone on an exotic island, cut off from reality and danger.

On their first day home the sky was a leaden gray, and the snow outside the ranch house lay in deep drifts. Amber was going through her mail at Jake's desk while he sat beside her, listening to the recorded telephone messages on his answering machine. He had the volume set very low so as not to disturb her.

At every call, the lines between his brows seemed to etch themselves more deeply into his dark face.

"Back to the real world," she said, sighing as she watched him.

"You're not kidding." He was drumming a pencil against the wooden desk. "I feel like I owe money to everybody in the world."

Amber slit open an envelope and gave an excited cry. She handed Jake the huge check from Sheila so that they could admire it together.

"That's wonderful, darling," he murmured warmly.

Jake listened to his next message and then pushed several buttons and listened again. Then again.

"Amber, I can't believe this!"

Some urgent element in his voice caught her attention. Her gaze jerked toward him. At first she thought he was upset, but then she realized he was grinning.

"Amber, this is a call from an old friend of mine in Denver. I helped him once when he was in a jam. Before we left he told me no, but now he says he's managed to scrape together the money I need to keep the resort afloat."

She placed her arms on his shoulders. "Oh, Jake, I'm so glad."

He pulled her closer. "Darling, I feel like the knot in my gut is starting to unravel. I didn't want to default on my interim financing. Some of my best friends have put every dime they have into this deal."

He punched the recorder again, but this time the call wasn't for him.

A raw whisper hacked through Amber's joy like an ax severing a vital artery. "Mrs. Kassidy... you know what we want."

Amber's hand fell away from Jake's shoulder. It was as if a door had opened and an icy wind had blasted into the cozy living room. She started to get up, but Jake's hand closed around her arm.

He was about to punch the button again and listen to the message a second time.

Amber's hand gripped his. "No!"

"But, darling..."

"It's nothing, Jake. Really. Just a joke."

"Then why aren't we laughing?"

This time when she pulled away from him, he let her go, but she was aware of him watching her as she went to the window and stared out at the cold white world.

She was trapped! No matter how much money she sent Don, it would never be enough. No matter what she did or where she went, the men who were after her would find her. She should never have married Jake, never have deluded herself that she and Jake had a chance of being happy together as long as these men wanted money from her.

It was only a matter of time before they came after her.

The call had brought a new tension between Jake and Amber. He wanted her to confide in him, and she couldn't. She was almost glad when he had to go to Denver on business.

One bright, snowy afternoon after she'd worked all day, Amber drove over to visit Serena. Serena and Paula were in the kitchen. The table was piled high with publicity mailings and both women were licking and stamping. Amber sat down and joined them.

When Paula left to start supper, Serena said, "Amber darling, your marriage to Jake was the best thing that ever happened to me."

Amber didn't dare lift her eyes from the long white envelope she was holding.

"You see," Serena continued, "for years I thought I was in love with Jake."

Amber froze. "Serena, maybe it would be better if you didn't tell me this."

Serena laid her hand gently on top of Amber's. "No, Amber. I, too, thought that once, but now I'm sure we need to talk this out. Jake doesn't want me. He wants you. I'm sure he's falling in love with you. And I'm glad."

Amber glanced up, uncertain. "What makes you think he's falling in love?"

"Darling, I grew up with him. I know all the signs. He's so possessive. So intense." Serena's fingers tightened around Amber's cold hand. "Please believe me when I say that, more than anything, I want you both to be happy."

"But I thought..." Amber's weak voice trailed away.

"So did I. Oh, Amber, I owe you so much, darling. Your coming here, your fighting to be independent, are responsible for my new happiness."

"I don't understand."

"I guess it's easy to fall into the habit of accepting false answers about one's life. For a long time I blamed all my dissatisfactions on not marrying Jake. You see, I was still infatuated with him when I married Hamlin. Now I realize that I did marry the right man. Years ago, Jake thought I married Hamlin for money, and maybe in part I did marry him out of a need for security. But there was more to it than that. Jake dominated me, and we always fought. Hamlin was willing to let me be myself."

"If I've played any part in helping you find your-self, Serena, I'm glad."

Their eyes met with new understanding. For the first time in months Serena seemed relaxed. Her eyes were sparkling with the inner warmth that comes from be-ing fulfilled and in love.

"Be happy, Amber. Make Jake happy. He's always been so alone."

Amber fell silent. All she could think of were the se-crets she had deliberately kept from him.

As Amber drove home she decided that, no matter how it terrified her, she had to be completely honest with Jake about her past, though she knew that by do-ing so she risked everything.

When she neared their ranch house, she saw a strange blue car in the drive. She gave the car no serious thought, figuring Jake probably had had a problem and had rented a car.

Careful to step over the patches of slick ice, she made her way to the front door. As she reached for the door-knob, the door was pulled roughly open. Her heart lurched sickeningly.

Framed in the doorway was the blond plumpish man with the thin yellow hair and the sunburned forehead.

She looked into his pale eyes and felt herself shiver.

He licked his lips and gave her a cold wet smile. A startled breath paralyzed her throat and choked off her scream.

No! It couldn't be!

But it was!

He began to laugh, and when she would have run, he grabbed her and jerked her viciously inside.

Amber became aware of the other two men in the house. A great, dark, menacing hulk of a man towered over Don, who looked white and scared as he sat slumped in Jake's recliner. When Don lifted his gaze to hers, she saw that half his face was purple with bruises.

"Oh, Don." She ran to him. "You're hurt."

"I told these guys to leave you alone, Amber," he said weakly. "If they would only wait a little longer, I could pay them every cent I owe them. I've got a new deal that's—"

"We've heard that line before," said the blond man.

His whispery voice was overwhelmingly frightening to Amber.

"Your wife has at least made some attempt to pay us," came that dreadful whisper. Pale, terrible eyes left Don and probed her.

"I'm not his wife!"

The blond man moved toward her, stalking her. He studied the room, then her.

She backed away until she was against the wall, and he came after her. Her fingers slid against the paneling. There was no escape. She stared at him in dumb alarm. It took superhuman effort to force herself to deal with this inhuman person. "I—remarried. I want to make a new life for myself. You've got to quit threatening me. P-please."

"Pay us, then."

"I can't!"

"Oh, but you can." Again those pale, dreadful eyes studied the room. Again they came back to her chalk-white face. "You've obviously married a man with money."

"I can't ask him."

Her tormentor grabbed her then, gripping her arm below the elbow in an iron grasp that produced shattering pain. He said almost good-naturedly, "You *will* ask him, though."

She was quivering and desperately frightened as he jerked her close against his body. He pulled out a gun, and she began to tremble.

From behind them came a deadly quiet drawl she recognized instantly.

"Ask me what?" Jake demanded.

The blond man pivoted, holding Amber even more tightly than before.

Jake's face hardened when he saw the gun and recognized the man.

"Your wife owes our organization a great deal of money."

Jake's eyes swept to Amber, and his forbidding look filled her with distress. He came nearer until he was so close he could have touched her, but he didn't touch her. He just stared at her wordlessly. Her heart was in her eyes, but she was as incapable of speech as he.

"Jake, I was going to tell you," she finally managed.

Jake's mouth twisted in a grimace of controlled agony. His eyes moved to the man holding her. "How much do you want?"

The blond man named a figure that would take everything Jake had and more.

"Let her go and clear out of here," Jake said, "and I'll pay you."

"But—"

"Let her go," Jake demanded. "I'll give you my lawyer's phone number in Denver. I'll make the arrangements through him Monday."

The blond man released Amber reluctantly. "If you're lying, we'll be back."

Amber sank against the wall, too weak to move, too shamed to speak.

After the three men left, Jake went to the bar and splashed scotch into a glass.

She watched miserably as he bolted it and poured himself another.

"Jake," she began quietly, "you'll be ruined. What about your friends? Do you have the right to jeopardize their money, too?"

He shot her a cold look, then turned his head from her in stubborn silence.

"If you do this, you'll tarnish your reputation," she cried. "I can't let you destroy yourself because of me."

"You don't have any choice."

"Jake, listen—"

He slammed his glass down on the bar. "No! You listen! Get this through your head, Amber. I don't want to talk about it. Not to you. Not tonight. I want to be left alone—completely alone! Do you understand!"

She had no more words for him. No tears. Silently she left the room and climbed the stairs to their bedroom. She took a long bath, and still he neither left the house nor came upstairs. She knew he was down there hating her for destroying everything he'd worked so hard for. Darkness fell, and though she hadn't eaten anything since lunch, she didn't dare go downstairs.

At last she got into bed and lay there, listening, waiting, hearing every nuance of the silence as a still cold night settled upon the valley. After a while she dozed, then awoke with a start.

She knew it was late. The house was dark and silent, but Jake had not come to bed.

Summoning her courage, she went downstairs to see if he was all right. Quietly she opened the den door a crack and peered in. The decanter of scotch on the bar was still almost full, the glass beside it empty. At least he hadn't drunk himself into a stupor because of her.

Jake was sprawled in a twisted position across the couch, which was much too small to accommodate her, much less a man his size. When she pushed against the door, it creaked, and he came awake instantly.

She longed to run into his arms, to beg his forgiveness, but something in his gaze stopped her dead on the threshold. He stared at her with steady dark eyes that were heavy with fatigue and worry.

Though the room lay in shadows, the light was sufficient to show him the figure hovering at the door. She wore nothing but a thin nightgown, and he could see the silhouette of her body. Male need, intense and swift, turned his blood to flame. She sure as hell knew every trick in the book!

Shock, and the savage beating of a pulse in his throat, made his low tone tight and constrained. "I thought you were in bed."

"I came down to see if you were all right." Her voice was slow and husky.

"As if you care."

She rushed into the room and he arose from the couch. They came together in the center of the dark stillness.

"I'm your wife," she said, reaching out hesitantly, touching him, placing her arms around his neck. "Of course I care."

The scent of her enveloped him. Her fingertips felt like fire against his skin, and all the hot dangerous feelings he didn't want to have for her came alive.

If only she hadn't touched him. If only her skin weren't so soft, her lips so provocatively near his own.

Maybe he could have resisted her. He had warned her, hadn't he? Told her to go away and leave him alone?

His blood had begun to beat violently.

"Yes, damn you, you're my wife!" His hand had become entangled in her hair, and he jerked her head back. A dull light shone on her ashen face, and he saw her sudden fear of him. Gently he traced the softness of her cheek with the back of his hand. "I bought and paid for you. Never have I paid so dearly for a woman." Never had a woman been so dear. "Laugh at me, darling. I have it coming. I really believed you when you said you wanted to be independent, when you were concerned about me spending money on you."

She went even whiter. "You shouldn't have agreed to pay them all that money. You don't owe them. I do."

He laughed softly—at his own stupidity. He had known she was trouble. He had known he should never have married her, but he had been irresistibly drawn. He was furious with her, with himself, but now his pulse was throbbing, and he could scarcely breathe. His fingers closed around the soft flesh of her upper arm and he dragged her down to the carpet. "I had to pay off those hoods because I couldn't risk what they might do to you."

Amber tried to turn away, but he wouldn't let her. As he stared into her pale, drawn face, he realized she was everything to him. He'd risked his life and every dime he had to save her, yet she would neither trust him nor confide in him. Had she only married him for his money? Did he mean nothing to her? Suddenly, because of his own hurt, he had an overpowering impulse to hurt her, punish her. "Tell me, darling," he snarled softly, "did you come down tonight to make sure I got my money's worth?"

She cried out as he reached for her and pulled her hard against his aroused body.

"Don't touch me," she pleaded, shamed and humiliated by what he'd said as well as by what she could read in his eyes.

"Don't touch you," he mocked, smiling nastily. "I bought you, remember?"

"Jake, please listen to me. I love you. I wasn't using you."

He seemed not to hear her; he pulled her inexorably beneath his great male body. She felt the heat of him, the eager trembling of his hands as he ripped her nightgown from her body.

"Please—"

"You shouldn't have come down here," he muttered. His eyes were so hard and dark they seemed almost black.

His weight crushed her beneath his chest, and his rough fingers seized her chin and lifted it upward. Then his mouth was on hers. She felt his tongue thrust insolently between her teeth. His passion raged out of control. He kissed her mouth, her face, her ears, her throat. She lay beneath him, sighing, breathless, lost. Then he paused and undressed.

"Don't do this, Jake. You'll only make me hate you."

"I'd rather have your hate than nothing. That's all I had before."

She was frantic to make him understand. "No, Jake," she whispered. "I loved you."

His face darkened, closed. "Call it whatever you like. You married me because you were in trouble." His eyes were as hard as diamonds. "Not because you loved me."

"Jake, I tried to tell you there were reasons why I shouldn't get involved with you. I don't want you to pay those men. I'll go away."

He clenched her more tightly against his taut body. He felt the burning softness of her skin against his. She felt his hands in her hair, pressing against her scalp through the red-gold strands as he held her to him. "They would only track you down. Besides, how would I live without you? I'd rather lose everything else I owned than risk—" He broke off, not wanting her to realize how his voice shook with desire.

He lowered his mouth, and his rough kisses wove a spell that was unimagined ecstasy. Her blood was pounding through her veins like a scalding tide. She wanted to talk to him, to make him understand, but every time she parted her lips his mouth was there ravishing hers. Every time he kissed her, her will to reason with him dissolved.

His love-making was deliciously dizzying. She was aware of every point where their naked bodies touched. His curly chest hair rasped against the softness of her satin breasts, arousing them until they peaked with longing. She felt the muscled hardness of his stomach and abdomen, the thrusting maleness of his thighs against her hips.

He was man and she was woman. And the need of him surpassed all other needs.

It was no use trying to explain to him, she thought weakly. No use. He wouldn't believe her.

Not that she blamed him. Vaguely she realized she should have told him the truth from the beginning. Now it was too late. Because of her he would be ruined financially. His name would become a thing of shame to him. There was no way she would ever be able to win his trust, and without that she could never win his love. In time, even his passion would die.

His molten body claimed hers, and she arched against him, surrendering to a passion that brought them both to shattering ecstasy.

Later, when it was over, he moved away from her. She knew he was studying her in the darkness, thinking, wondering. Neither of them could find the courage to speak. At last he levered himself off the carpet, pulled on his clothes, and arose.

Amber watched him in silence. She felt exhausted, helpless, defeated.

"I'm going out," he said. "I need some time to think." His voice was curt, his eyes dark and remote.

She heard the faint jingle of his keys as he pulled them from his pocket.

She closed her eyes, turning away from him. There seemed nothing she could do. Nothing she could say.

There was a rush of cold air, and then the door banged behind him. She heard his truck, and then there was nothing but the dark and the cold and the silence.

She was alone. As she had always been alone. Cut off from love.

She curled into a tight ball of pain.

Her marriage was as dead as ashes.

Chapter Fifteen

An aquamarine surf lazily washed sugar-white sand. The silken petals of a scarlet hibiscus blossom fluttered in the faint breeze.

On her way to Angela's jewelry shop, Amber's skirt brushed the blood-red flowers, but she scarcely noted their beauty, just as she had failed to notice the brilliant tropical winter afternoon. She was too upset even to feel the unseasonable heat, to think or feel anything other than numbness and loss.

She pushed the brass door of the luxurious jewelry shop open and stepped inside, into the floral-scented womb of pink and gold that was her friend Angela's domain. Amber's heels sank soundlessly into the deep carpet. Angela looked up briefly from across the room, caught her friend's dark mood and nodded in mute understanding before vanishing into the back of the shop.

Dear Angela. What other friend would have been so understanding? She'd taken Amber into her home, asked no questions, demanded no answers.

Two days ago Amber had flown from Colorado to the Bahamas, and each day the pain inside her seemed to grow rather than lessen. Every part of her ached for Jake, but she had run from him, just as once she had run from this island.

Odd, how alien it all felt now, this place she'd once considered her home. She was in the midst of a balmy paradise, but she longed for snow-clad mountains, for the warmth of strong brown arms holding her close, for the warmth of jade-green eyes, for that special smile of Jake's that was hers alone.

Was there no place on earth where she could hide from the sorrow in her own soul?

Her hands began to shake, and the blue slip of paper she had been clenching fell from her fingers to the carpet. She gave a little cry of pain as she knelt to retrieve it.

The slanting black script blurred as Amber studied the check Don had written her yesterday.

Yesterday... Was it only yesterday that she had hoped so frantically that this insignificant scrap of paper could save her marriage? She gulped in a deep breath. Then she set the check on the counter and stared out the window because it almost made her physically ill to look at it. It symbolized the hopelessness of her feelings.

As soon as she'd arrived in the Bahamas, Don had looked her up, saying in that blithe, breezy way of his, "Baby, now that I'm back on top, I can repay you the money I owe you." When she had only looked at him, wondering how his financial picture could change so dramatically almost overnight, he'd insisted, "Hey, I know this is a shock, but you know how it is with me, babe. One day I'm up, the next I'm down. I told you I was going to pull myself out of this.'' Amber had begun to shake her head hysterically, refusing the money. ''Of course you'll take it. I owe it to you. Hell, babe, I owe you my life. Those guys play pretty rough. Thanks for everything. I always told you I'd pull off another successful real estate deal, didn't I?''

She listened in stunned silence, watched blankly as he stuffed the check into her purse because she was too lifeless to reach out and accept it. Then, before she could either ask questions or protest, he'd left her, returning to his world of casinos and high-flying deals. If she hadn't found his check in her purse later, she would never have believed he'd been real.

Eventually, when she'd realized what the money could mean to Jake, she'd rushed to the phone and tried to call him, first at his ranch and then at his construction site in Steamboat Springs. A man had taken her messages in Steamboat Springs, and later, when she'd called again, the man had coldly informed her that Jake wasn't interested in her money. Nor had Jake returned her calls.

She had sat by the phone all day, hoping against hope.

Amber lifted the check from the counter. It was ironic that Don had repaid her one day after her marriage ended.

What did she care about having his money now that she had lost Jake? What did she care about achieving independence? About being somebody? It seemed to her that nothing would ever again have any meaning.

She folded the check and put it in her purse. Tomorrow she would mail Jake the money Don had given her.

Tomorrow she would try to summon the courage to face the fact that she would have to live the rest of her life without the only man she could ever love.

There were tears in her eyes, but she wiped them away with the back of her hand. She was afraid if she let herself cry she wouldn't be able to stop.

Suddenly she had to get out of the jewelry shop.

She was suffocating. She was dying.

It was no use fooling herself that by staying she was helping Angela.

Amber decided to go down to the beach and watch the wind and the waves.

Liar!

All she wanted was to be alone so that she could think of Jake.

Passionflowers dripped like exquisite purple jewels from lush, towering shrubbery. Jake didn't even see them as he walked quickly toward the beach.

Above, a gull soared and dived, screaming.

The path turned abruptly, and he saw Amber. He stopped in the shadows of the tress to watch her before she saw him.

She was standing waist-deep in the water, sifting the sparkling water-droplets through her fingers, her thick fiery mane piled on top of her head in a tangled bundle while unruly wisps escaped and blew about her neck. There was a new stillness about her, an uncharacteristic forlornness that caught at Jake's heart.

She came out of the sea, her body glistening, and she gave her head a quick shake that sent pins flying, and a long wave of fire showering over her shoulders.

If he hadn't been so wrenched by his own agony it would have 'angered Jake to find her thus, swimming, idling away her time as if she hadn't a care in the world. While he... When he'd found her gone, he hadn't known whether she was dead or alive. Whether she'd walked out on him of her own accord or been abducted by the hoods who had demanded money from him.

Was she that heartless? That indifferent? Had she walked out on him and never given him a second thought? He'd gone wild when he'd come home and found her gone. There hadn't been the slightest clue as to where she'd gone.

Then yesterday, at last, she'd called, and he'd known where she was. Her idea had been to pay him off. He'd served his purpose. Well, damn her. She wasn't going to get off that easily. If she was through with him because she had no further use for him, she could at least tell him to his face.

She turned then and saw him, her expression lighting in recognition, surprise, and then... Her eyes widened in fear. She tensed.

A knife sliced through his gut, but he ignored the pain and walked briskly toward her through the deep sand. He wanted to hate her.

She came out of the water. Her face was very white, very vulnerable. Inanely, he found himself feeling sorry for her. Sand filled his shoes, and he kicked them off.

She was smiling at him now, uncertainly, a tentative shy smile of disbelief and joy. The pain from the knife in his gut lessened.

His gaze trailed over her wet body. The clinging bikini was the most erotic costume imaginable. She was naked except for two strips of dripping cloth barely covering her golden body. He watched water-droplets run down her flushed skin. He could almost feel the heat of her.

He had lost her—yet never had he wanted her more.

He felt on fire, and he hated the power she had over him. He wanted to pull her into his arms, to crush her breasts against his rib cage, to devour that pink rose-petal mouth with his lips. Desire gnawed at him like a savage beast.

When she came up to him and stood so close he could have touched her, he didn't dare. Her eyes were huge. Did he only imagine that a slight tremor shook her body?

He couldn't say anything. He just stood there like an awkward kid, staring at her with a wary, tortured intensity, memorizing every feminine detail. Thanking God that she was alive. Loving her and hating himself all the more because he did.

He could feel the dampness of her in every pore of his body; he could smell the saltiness, the sea-flavor of her.

He started to say something, but emotion choked back his words. He felt stupid. Idiotic. He had a lot to tell her. What in the hell was wrong with him?

She sucked in a deep breath and gathered her courage. His handsome face was so dark and tense. "Why did you come, Jake?" she managed softly, her fear of him shuddering in the velvet sound.

"Maybe you should explain why the hell you walked out on me?" he managed at last, his voice a terse growl.

She looked away. Then her long-lashed eyes returned to his face. "Because...because...I thought that's what you wanted.

The sun shone on her coppery hair. He studied the luxuriant golden-red curls, the pouting fullness of her mouth, the pale perfection of her face. To him she was the most beautiful woman in the world, and the dearest. Why did she seem so fragile, so vulnerable?

"You thought I wanted you gone?" he asked in a harsh, incredulous tone.

"You were so mad."

"Hell, yes, I was mad," he admitted raggedly. "I thought you married me to use me." His green eyes raked her.

Amber wet her lips. She felt so helpless, so unable to explain. It was as if her whole life hung in the balance. Was he really giving her one last chance? Was it possible that he still cared? At last she summoned the courage to begin.

"But I didn't want to use you, Jake. I love you. That's the only reason I married you. If you can't believe anything else, believe that. I didn't want you to get messed up in my life. That's why I fought my feelings for you so hard in the beginning. But in the end I couldn't stop myself. I married you because I couldn't live without you. I kept childishly hoping that maybe my problems would go away. Maybe Don would be able to make some money. I know it all sounds mixed up now, and that's because I'm all mixed up and can't put my feelings into the right words. I don't know what I thought, really. I just know that I couldn't *not* marry you, Jake. I loved you too much. I..."

She stopped, and stared earnestly into his eyes. Her whole heart had been in her words.

"I love you, too," he said simply.

"Then..."

His heart ached with a happiness such as he had never known before. "Then nothing else matters. Not the money. Not your failure to confide in me," he said, more gently than he'd ever spoken to her before. "Somehow, we'll find each other."

They were in each other's arms, she dripping from her swim, he still in his suit and tie. He drew her to him for a deep, long kiss. He felt a ridiculous, crazy, youthful elation.

His voice was husky against her mouth. "I didn't know where you'd gone until you called yesterday."

"I didn't think you'd want to know."

As if he wanted to press her inside his body, he hugged her closer. His cotton dress-shirt stuck to her wet skin. She could feel his heart pounding.

"You little fool. I've been crazy with worry. I thought maybe those guys had taken you." He kissed her hair, then her lips again. "Then when Roger told me you called yesterday and all you talked about was money, I went crazy. I didn't care about the money. I just wanted you back. I was too afraid to talk to you on the phone. Too afraid I'd scare you, and you'd run some place where I couldn't find you. I had to come see you and talk to you face-to-face."

"Yesterday Don repaid me the money, Jake. I wanted you to have it. I wanted to save you, your reputation, the resort.

"Darling, the money doesn't matter to me. I realized that when you walked out. Without you in my life, I wanted to die. I've been putting too much importance on the wrong goals for a long time. I wanted to be a financial success because I felt I had to be to get the woman I wanted. I realize now that that kind of success isn't nearly as important as I thought it was. If I had all the money in the world and lost you, I would have nothing."

"I guess we both learned the same lesson," she murmured. "A long time ago I thought having things meant I was loved."

"I don't care if I lose everything," he said, "now that I have you."

"Well, you're going to get the money back." Gently she pushed him away. "And when you do, will you be able to save the resort?"

"To hell with the resort," he whispered, pulling her lips against his own. "Haven't you been listening to me?"

She brought two fingers to his mouth and pushed him away. "Jake, I know the resort's important to you, and I want to know if there's a chance you can save it."

"It'll be tough going, but I'll probably be able to work through all the problems." His grip tightened on her body. "It's you I want. You, I love. You, I don't want to live without."

"Oh, Jake . . ." She felt him trembling.

"I love you, Amber. When you were gone, and I didn't know where you were, I felt like a part of me had died. It was worse than anything I've ever gone through before. I'll do anything, if only you'll come back to me." His voice was hoarse and charged with emotion.

"Jake..." Her throat was suddenly tight. Because of her love-starved childhood, she had never really believed that he loved her, that he might need her as she needed him. "Do you really mean it?"

"Mean it?" He stared at her in wonder. "I wanted you from the first moment I saw you on that cliff. Since that afternoon you've haunted my every waking thought. I don't know how I ever could have believed you married me to use me. And I was a beast that last night. I was afraid that maybe you would hate me for that."

"You were hurt and angry."

His arms were around her, holding her so tightly she could scarcely breathe. His face came down to rest against her forehead. Amber's arms went around his waist. He felt so solid, so right. She knew she never wanted to be far from the sweetness of his embrace.

At last, for the first time in her life she felt loved, truly loved, and she was filled with a glorious sense of peace and happiness and rapture. Love was everything she had ever wanted and so much more.

"Jake, I never wanted to use you," Amber said. "I wanted to solve my problems without your help. And I did try. Even though I really didn't have anything to do with Don's bad investments, I felt responsible because I was his wife when he made them. And I did want all the things his money could buy. So I mailed him all the money I made. The reason I didn't tell you the truth was because for the first time in my life I was fighting to be independent, and also because I was afraid, not only for Don and myself, but for you.

"Oh, Amber, I'm proud of you and deeply in love with you. Maybe now we've both learned that we're not alone anymore, that we have someone we can confide in."

They held onto each other tightly. "Darling," he said, "you're the only woman I've every truly loved, and I'll never let you go."

She brought his brown hand to her lips and kissed it gently, tantalizingly. Her mouth touched warm metal, and she paused.

Glittering on his finger was the golden wedding band she'd made for him.

She smiled. "So you really do intend to belong to me forever?"

He lifted her in his arms. "I'll give you your answer in deeds, not words."

She laughed. "In broad daylight?" She was trembling in anticipation.

He pulled her beneath the deep purple shade where the passionflowers bloomed in profusion. He broke the stem of a blossom and tucked the jewel-flower behind her ear.

"Take me home, Jake," she murmured. "Oh, take me home."

The rich perfume of the flowers enveloped them. A salt-kissed wind caressed them.

"Later," he whispered. "Later."

"Much later," she sighed, languidly melting into the heat of sinewy muscle and bone.

He kissed her, the fairy-tale girl, whose dreams had come true at last.

*   *   *   *   *

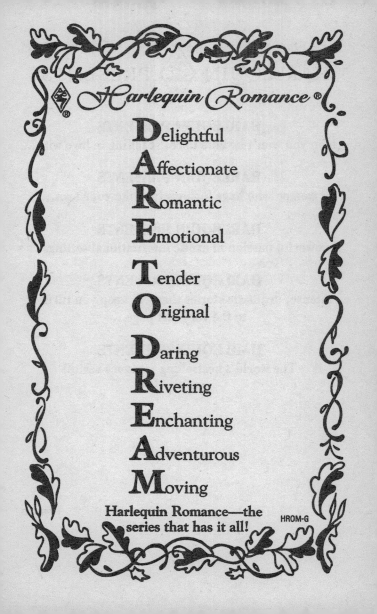

Harlequin Romance ®

Delightful
Affectionate
Romantic
Emotional

Tender
Original

Daring
Riveting
Enchanting
Adventurous
Moving

**Harlequin Romance—the
series that has it all!**

HROM-G

HARLEQUIN PRESENTS®

HARLEQUIN PRESENTS
men you won't be able to resist falling in love with...

HARLEQUIN PRESENTS
women who have feelings just like your own...

HARLEQUIN PRESENTS
powerful passion in exotic international settings...

HARLEQUIN PRESENTS
intense, dramatic stories that will keep you turning
to the very last page...

HARLEQUIN PRESENTS
The world's bestselling romance series!

Harlequin® Historical

If you're a serious fan of historical romance,
then you're in luck!

Harlequin Historicals brings you
stories by bestselling authors, rising new stars
and talented first-timers.

Ruth Langan & Theresa Michaels
Mary McBride & Cheryl St. John
Margaret Moore & Merline Lovelace
Julie Tetel & Nina Beaumont
Susan Amarillas & Ana Seymour
Deborah Simmons & Linda Castle
Cassandra Austin & Emily French
Miranda Jarrett & Suzanne Barclay
DeLoras Scott & Laurie Grant...

You'll never run out of favorites.

Harlequin Historicals...they're too good to miss!

HARLEQUIN®

I N T R I G U E ®

THAT'S INTRIGUE—DYNAMIC ROMANCE AT ITS BEST!

Harlequin Intrigue is now bringing you more—more men and mystery, more desire and danger. If you've been looking for thrilling tales of contemporary passion and sensuous love stories with taut, edge-of-the-seat suspense—then you'll *love* Harlequin Intrigue!

Every month, you'll meet four new heroes who are guaranteed to make your spine tingle and your pulse pound. With them you'll enter into the exciting world of Harlequin Intrigue—where your life is on the line and so is your heart!

Harlequin Intrigue—we'll leave you breathless!

SPECIAL EDITION

Stories of love and life, these powerful
novels are tales that you can identify with—
romances with "something special" added in!

Fall in love with the stories of authors such
as **Nora Roberts, Diana Palmer, Ginna Gray**
and many more of your special favorites—as
well as wonderful new voices!

Special Edition brings you
entertainment for the heart!

SSE-GEN

LOOK FOR OUR FOUR FABULOUS MEN!

Each month some of today's bestselling authors bring
four new fabulous men to Harlequin American Romance.
Whether they're rebel ranchers, millionaire power brokers
or sexy single dads, they're all gallant princes—and
they're all ready to sweep you into lighthearted fantasies
and contemporary fairy tales where anything is possible
and where all your dreams come true!

You don't even have to make a wish...Harlequin American
Romance will grant your every desire!

Look for Harlequin American Romance wherever Harlequin
books are sold!